Bear's Heart

Bear's Heart

The Calhouns & Campbells of Cold Canyon Ranch

Jane Porter

Bear's Heart

Tule Publishing First Printing, July 2024

The Tule Publishing, Inc.

First Publication by Tule Publishing 2024

Cover design by Lee Hyat Designs

ISBN: 978-1-962707-06-0

Dedication

For Sinclair Sawhney and Kelly Hunter
Brilliant writers, gifted editors and beloved friends

Chapter One

JOSIE CALHOUN SQUINTED against the late afternoon sunlight, studying the front of the big, beautiful Montana log cabin.

The ranch house, completed four years ago, had been built for a man who had everything. For a man who *thought* he had everything.

The twenty-three-year-old designer-in-training stood at the edge of the sweeping gravel driveway, holding her breath, feeling the awful weight, and truth, of this house. Of what this grand sprawling house represented. It was to have been a celebration of a Montana man's accomplishments. This was his success story. His reward. It was also a house that had never been lived in until now.

Josie hadn't been part of the design team that built it, but she'd been aware that her firm had created the luxurious home, turning Bear Anderson's wish list and dreams into reality. He'd been an integral part of the plans and she'd poured over them in the office because Bear Anderson was huge, a local hero. Everybody knew him, even if they hadn't met him. For years, the state and local papers faithfully covered his career, keeping the public up to date on his success in the PRCA, and then later on the Professional Bull Rider tour.

It was on the PBR tour that it changed. She, like everyone else in Montana, knew the moment life as he knew it vanished. It had only taken six and a half seconds in Tulsa to destroy a life.

No one thought a catastrophic accident would happen to Braden "Bear" Anderson. The Clyde Park native, a three-time national bull-riding champion, had never even been seriously hurt before—or if he had, he'd kept his injuries to himself, competing as if he was invincible.

And in the public's mind, he was. Bear was Bear. A legend. He earned his nickname as a skinny freckled faced ten-year-old when he took on a grizzly during a family fishing trip outside West Yellowstone, distracting the bear who'd gotten a little too interested in Braden's eight-year-old sister.

Montanans loved courage. Bravery. And they loved that one of their own would challenge a grizzly and live to tell about it.

So, Bear became a hero long before he ever won his first big belt buckle. It went without saying, it just about broke everyone's heart when that rank bull came crashing down on him in Tulsa and wouldn't let him up.

Folks watching the event that night—whether there at the Bank of Oklahoma Center or home watching live—thought the bull had killed Bear. People wept as he was carried unconscious from the arena and the other PBR cowboys took off their hats, formed a circle and got down on a knee to pray. *Please, Lord, don't take Bear.*

God heard. He spared Bear's life, but Bear was done riding and competing. Done walking, too. No way he could walk, not with what that bull did to his spinal cord.

It'd taken tough, fearless Bear Braden Anderson two and a half years to accept that there was nothing else the medical community could do for him. His bull riding career was behind him. He'd left his place outside Nashville and was returning to Montana, and the luxurious cabin built for him on his Clyde Park ranch with the jagged, snow-capped Crazies for a view.

Josie blinked against the glaring reflection of the summer sun off the long metal ramp. The ramp hid the handsome log cabin's big front porch. The two-story, five-bedroom home had been built with reclaimed lumber, which had cost a fortune, but Bear hadn't cared. Bear had been making good money on the circuit and even better money through sponsors and endorsements. Everyone loved a success story, and Bear's was downright mythical.

Now Bear was back, broken, and as he'd said in a late-night phone call to the design firm's answering service, he couldn't even pee in his multimillion-dollar dream home because his wheelchair couldn't fit through any of the bathroom doors on the main floor.

Which was why Josie was here. To get changes made. Fast.

But before she could even get to the interior modifications, she'd be sure to have something done about the ramp out front, aware that Bear hated it.

The lead architect at the firm had tried explaining to Bear on the phone yesterday that it was just a temporary ramp, quickly constructed so Bear could get into his house, as there were three steps to the front porch, and six at the back, where the property sloped down. But Bear didn't care that it had been thrown together for his convenience. He hung up on the architect, and then one of the project managers. He refused to speak to the contractor who came out yesterday to meet him, and now Josie was here, not because there was no one else, but because she'd volunteered.

Her brother was in a wheelchair. She'd grown up watching him struggle. Accessibility wasn't an option. It was necessary. But it didn't have to be ugly, and she could see how the cheap aluminum ramp in front of his house upset him.

But there was more to it than compassion. Working on his house could fulfil her final design project requirement for her to graduate and, so far, her advisors hadn't signed off on a project and she was down to six months before graduation, six months to show her advisors—and future employers—what she could do.

Josie sucked in a breath for courage and called Bear.

He didn't answer.

He could have been sleeping, or he could just be sitting

inside ignoring her.

Josie drew another breath and phoned again. It rang and rang, and she was just about to think she'd end up in his voice mail again but suddenly he was there.

"Hello?" he said tersely.

"It is an ugly ramp," Josie said quickly. "I'm standing outside, in front of your house, and I can see why you hate the ramp. It's a monstrosity and everyone could have done better. We should have done better, Mr. Anderson."

"Who is this?" he asked after a moment, his voice deep, hoarse.

"Josie Calhoun."

"I don't recognize your name. Were you on my design team?"

"No."

"Then what are you doing here?"

"I'm an intern with the firm—"

"An *intern*?"

"Yes, an intern, but I also have more experience with universal design—"

"What does that mean?"

"I specialize in accessible design, and I'm here of my own volition. I'm here because I want to make it right, and I know I can."

"Are you the one standing in my yard?"

"I am."

He sighed, exasperated, and then the line went dead.

Josie glanced at her phone. He'd hung up on her.

But then the front door opened, and a shadow stretched across the porch. "You coming in?" The deep voice called, coming from the threshold.

Bear.

Josie swallowed hard, suddenly nervous, and clutched her notebook closer to her chest. "Coming," she said loudly, before quickly walking up the shiny silver ramp, her footsteps sounding like thunder on the aluminum surface.

BEAR ROLLED BACK from the door to let Josie Calhoun enter. He wasn't in a good mood. He hurt. But then he hurt all the time now. There was nothing right about being stuck in a chair. Stuck sitting. Even thirty-three months after the accident, he still felt trapped.

"Should I shut the door?" she asked.

Bear turned a little, glanced back at her. The white silver light reflecting off the ramp shone around her, creating a halo around her head, as if she were an angelic being instead of a Bozeman interior design intern who'd decided to pay a house call because she considered herself an expert. He appreciated confidence but today he wasn't in the mood for this … or her.

"Do you close your front door?" he snapped.

She quietly closed the door, but her expression was

amused more than intimidated.

"What?" he demanded.

"Nothing."

"You're *smiling*," he said tightly through gritted teeth.

"I'm just happy to be meeting you. I've followed your career since I was a little girl."

His narrowed gaze swept over her from head to foot. "You're still a little girl."

"Not super tall, no, but that's because I take after my mom." Her voice was light, friendly, as if determined to not be offended by his temper tantrum.

He knew he was having a temper tantrum, too. It'd been a terrible forty-eight hours, and Bear couldn't seem to shift his mood.

"What do you think you're going to do, Josie, when no one else at the firm could make things more accessible for me?"

"Let's put our cards on the table. There wasn't enough advance notice that you were returning—"

"It's my house. Why should I give advance notice if I want to come home?"

Her slim shoulders shrugged. "You are the one that wanted to get inside. And you are the one that requested the big porch and wide front steps. The house wasn't built with accessibility in mind. So now we need to do some retrofitting, but those changes take time."

He glanced away, jaw aching with suppressed fury. He'd

taken a hard fall last night trying to get through the narrow bathroom door to the toilet, and some falls bruised the ego, but this one had jarred his spine sending shockwaves of pain throughout his upper body. God only knew what his paralyzed lower half thought of it.

"I do want to help," she said quietly, her tone growing serious. "And I can. At least, as much as you'll let me."

He looked at her, his gaze sweeping over her, even as emotion filled him, nearly overwhelming him. Before he'd been hurt, he was the one helping others. Before Tulsa, he'd been the strong one, the one lifting others up, getting them through the hard times.

"What do you want from me?" he asked, voice dropping low.

"Your priority list. What needs to be fixed first, and so on."

"The bathroom."

"And then?"

"The kitchen."

She nodded. "How about I follow you? We can start with your bathroom or the kitchen. Your call."

"Let's start with the kitchen since it's the first room up."

"Sounds good." She dug into her purse and pulled out a tape measure. "Lead the way."

JOSIE WASN'T AS confident as she sounded. If anything, she was struggling not to be intimidated. She could feel Bear's tension. His frustration radiated off him in waves and every now and then there was a crack in his voice, a break that burrowed into her heart, taking up space.

He'd been through hell. She knew that. He was still going through hell, and she couldn't fix everything, but she could at least give him a space where he could be more comfortable and function without help. Independence was huge, especially for men like Bear.

Following him down the hall was deliberate, too. She wanted to see how he moved through his home, how he navigated the halls and spaces with his wheelchair. Wheelchairs weren't the same either. Some were wider, some set taller, some more manual. Some were electric, and she needed to see how he moved it and how much mobility he had, and it was all that would determine the choices she made.

Bear rolled past her, hands pushing the rims on his chair tires in quick impatient bursts. He wore a thick silver ring on his right hand, and as he pushed forward the ring tapped against the titanium rims. His chair was very new, and high performance, which meant lightweight, and durable, forgiving should it be dropped or kicked or worse.

Her family had a van for her brother but there was no van here. The only vehicle here—besides her own—was the orange and white Bronco out front.

"Is that your truck outside?" she asked, trailing after Bear as he led the way down the wide paneled hallway into an enormous kitchen with a soaring ceiling, rustic beams, handmade custom cabinets, and gleaming marble counters with tiled backsplash. The hood over the professional grade stove was hammered copper. Burnished copper pots hung from a beam near the stove and the line of stools at the island were covered in soft, supple butterscotch leather.

"Yes," he answered, coming to a stop on the far side of the kitchen. "Probably not the most practical vehicle, but it's been mine forever."

His right hand turned his chair around, facing her in front of the kitchen sink. The huge island stood between them; the island far too tall with him confined to a chair. There was no area for him to prep, nothing at the island that would allow him to roll under. Even washing dishes would require him to turn sideways and reach awkwardly into the deep sink.

"I like the colors," she said. "It's very seventies, and retro is in."

"Classic Broncos never went out."

She couldn't help smiling. He was so irritable and yet it was okay. She wasn't hurt by his brusqueness. If anything, his brusqueness told her just how much he was struggling.

Now he simply sat and waited, watching her.

Josie suspected this was a test, but she understood it. Very little worked for him in this gorgeous kitchen. It wasn't just that he couldn't roll under the sink or roll under a prep space, but the kitchen itself dwarfed him.

She walked the opposite way around the island, passing the refrigerator, around to the eight-burner stove with the big griddle in the center.

Everything in the kitchen was tall and oversized. Everything had been built on a massive masculine level. Even though Bear had once stood over six feet, he wasn't that man anymore. He had to operate from the height of one sitting, which meant counters needed to be lower, the sink and work stations needed to be open so he could roll under.

"I would replace your sink cabinets here," she said gesturing to the doors beneath the deep farmhouse sink. "If we remove the cabinets and shift the pipes back, you could roll right under, giving you better access to the faucets and the sink itself. I'd also downsize this island, which would give you more room to navigate around the appliances. You could keep some of this counter space, but here at this end I'd eliminate the under cabinets and drop the island surface to make it a proper work-prep area for you. The scale in here is impressive, but unfortunately, it doesn't suit your needs now."

She crossed back to the refrigerator and opened it, pleased to see that the refrigerator had adjustable shelves and drawers. The freezer also had flexible space. So, the fridge wouldn't need to be replaced. Just changing the island size would create more space for Bear to cook at the stove. He needed to be able to roll backward to open the oven doors, and needed space to pivot, shifting hot pans from one area of the stove to another.

But still, it was a tall stove. For his needs something smaller would be better.

"The stove is high," she said, "and I'm tempted to suggest that we remove the double ovens so the gas top can be lowered, but that depends on how much functionality you want and need." She hesitated. "And your budget, of course."

"I don't want to spend money I don't have to spend."

"Do you have a budget in mind?"

"I want to do as little in here as possible. I spent a fortune the first time getting it just the way I wanted. I'm not wanting to destroy what we did."

"But the layout doesn't work for you anymore—"

"It's fine."

"I don't think so. As a designer, I believe that functionality is even more important than aesthetics."

"If you cut down the island like you suggested, you'll have to replace flooring."

"I'm sure we can find an open box of material to patch, and you'd really be so much happier with a work or dining area that you could just roll under, whether you're prepping something or reading mail."

"Maybe." His brow furrowed. "Can you give me some numbers for what it would cost?"

"I can." She hesitated. "What about the sink?"

"I'll figure it out."

"You've only been back a few days. Won't you be frustrated when you try to use your kitchen?"

He lifted a dark eyebrow. "What makes you think I haven't?"

"The stove top is spotless. I doubt you've ever turned a burner on, never mind the oven."

"I've turned the oven on."

She remembered the stack of frozen pizza boxes in the freezer. "I suppose pizza counts."

His hard jaw eased. His lips curved faintly. "They don't have Door Dash out here, and I'm too far for Domino's."

She smiled back. "Well, a man's got to do what a man's got to do." Josie turned to the island again, studied the dimensions, making a mental note of where she'd cut the island, and where they'd need to patch the floor. "Just a thought, we could turn some of the island's lower cabinets into dish drawers. That way everything you need is easily available beneath the counters. I know a good carpenter who could do it in a couple of weeks, but you'd have to be patient with the process, since he'd probably be working you into his existing jobs."

"A couple weeks?"

"You want someone good," she said. "This is a custom kitchen with custom cabinetry. I'd only have the best finish carpenter work here."

"How disruptive would it be?"

"Depends on what we need to do for the bathroom. Should we look at that next?"

"That's where your skilled carpenter will be spending most of his time."

"On a scale of one to ten, how bad is the bathroom?"

"A seven or eight? You'll see in a moment what I mean. With enough maneuvering, I can shower and brush my teeth, but I'm not always successful. I've ended up on my butt more times than I care to admit." His lips twisted, a mocking smile. "Not that I haven't ended up on my butt plenty of times in the arena, but I got paid to fall. Here, not so much."

Again, Josie heard that thing in his voice that moved into her chest, making her heart ache. At least Jasper had grown up with his disability, not ever knowing a different life. Her dad had spent a life as a rancher and roofer, and he'd found it nearly impossible to come to terms with his accident. "Show me the way to your bedroom."

He gave her a look that put heat in her cheeks and made her face burn, a look that indicated he'd heard that before with very different intentions. Thank goodness, he didn't say anything, though, and pivoted the chair. She followed him through the wide kitchen doorway, back to the entry hall, where he turned left, rolling down a narrower hallway. The hallway was paneled, a warm rich wood that added warmth and style to an otherwise uninspiring space. Josie was surprised when he stopped, and leaned forward to turn the doorknob, pushing it open and rolling inside.

It was a small bedroom, with a full-size bed. There was no fancy bedframe or elegant linens, just a simple comforter spread over a mattress, the mattress on top of the box mattress, on a metal frame. The bed, though, was the same height as Bear's wheelchair which would make it easy to transfer. She suspected the wide nightstand was also there for leverage, should he need it. Except for the bed and nightstand, there was no other furniture in the room, and she knew why. He wouldn't be able to turn in the room if there had been a chair or desk. Throw rugs would just tangle him up. The room was empty and plain so he could get around. But it didn't have to be that colorless. It could be so much better.

"The bathroom is in here," he said gruffly, passing what she imagined was a tiny built in closet, to push open a door, revealing a small bathroom with a tub-shower combination, a built in vanity, and a toilet. A hospital style shower chair sat inside the tub. The shower head was a handheld device and it dangled into the tub.

Bear made it through the bathroom doorway, but his rims scraped on one side of the frame. She glanced down, seeing the scuffmarks and paint that had been scraped away, and then a hole in the drywall that clearly shouldn't be there.

"Was there always a handheld shower head in here?" she asked, ignoring the hole and focusing on what was important now.

"A neighbor put it in for me," he said.

Her attention shifted to the tiny sink. This sink, like the one in the kitchen, would work for him if he rolled up sideways and leaned forward, but she didn't know how much flexibility he had in his spine, or strength in his pelvis and hips. The ideal situation would be a roll under sink with no pipes in the way. Knee clearance needed to be at least twenty-seven inches high, and close to fifteen inches deep to accommodate his chair and knees—and he had long legs.

The towel bars should also be moved, and the toilet itself needed to be higher. She didn't know if he'd want a grab bar on one side. Jasper needed two grab bars, but she'd become aware in the past few months that some people wanted to downplay their different requirements, not wanting a home to look *handicapped.*

"You don't have a lot of room in here," she said finally, thinking as he transferred his chair would knock the sink, the toilet, the tub. There would be a lot of bumping around.

"It's frustrating," he agreed. "A bigger door would help."

"But you need more than just a couple inches for the doorway. You need to be able to move and turn. This isn't good space for you, not as your main bathroom."

"My only one," he corrected. "The guest bath off the entry is just a powder bath sort of thing. I can't even get my casters through that door, and well, obviously upstairs is off limits."

She faced him. "You have an enormous house here, and you can't use most of it. Wouldn't it be easier to sell this one, and find something that works better for you?"

He stiffened, broad shoulders squaring. "This *is* my home."

She heard his sharpness, but then, she'd been expecting it. But she had to ask. It was important to ask. "What you need then is a proper main suite downstairs. I'd need to see more of the house to know if you have space to convert, or if you'd have to build new—" She lifted a hand to stop his interruption. "A master on the main level would change everything for you."

"It would mean a huge remodel."

"You'd have to move out for a number of months, yes."

"Where would I go?"

"That's a good question."

His expression darkened. "I've spent years living in hospitals and facilities that weren't my home. I want to be home."

"I understand," she said softly. "I also understand this is your house, but it's clearly not home right now. You're not comfortable, or happy, here."

"I just want a bathroom that works for me."

"I want that for you, too. But the only way to do that is to enlarge this doorway and try to grab some space to give you a proper bathroom."

"What about when I want to sell this place? If it's full of

special accommodations for me, it won't work for those … unlike me."

"Just because you have a more accessible home doesn't mean it will be unattractive to buyers. If anything, having a bedroom suite on the main floor will be appealing to most."

His jaw worked. "You make it sound so easy."

"When you know the right people, I can safely promise you a good renovation experience, but demoing a bathroom always takes time. There are permits to be pulled and inspections to be made. We probably couldn't even get started for a good month—"

"That's too long."

"I suppose we could get some small changes done to try to tide you over."

Bear shook his head, clearly unhappy with what he was hearing. "I can't do months of this. I can't."

"In Bozeman, there are a number of long-term hotel options, and they'd have accessible suites."

He opened his mouth and then closed it. "I'll see you out."

She nodded, aware that he was disappointed, and his disappointment was heavy.

"The changes sound daunting, Mr. Anderson, but the good news is that once the remodel is done, this house will feel like you. It'll be your home again."

He opened the front door. "I don't know if that's possible."

She picked up her purse from the hall table, putting the measuring tape and notepad in one pocket and drawing out her business card folder from another. "Think about your options, and what you want to do," she said, placing her business card on the table. "These decisions are yours, and yours alone. But if I can help, I want to."

JOSIE CLIMBED INTO her small SUV and carefully backed into the driveway and then shifted into drive and pulled away from Bear's house, thinking it was possible Braden Anderson had earned his nickname not from fighting a bear, but from resembling a bear.

He was tough. Hard. Hurt.

But she could handle him. Braden Bear Anderson didn't scare her.

Hard to be scared of someone that made her breath catch. He was gorgeous. His back might have been shattered, but the good Lord had spared his face.

There was a reason local girls had been falling at Bear's feet since junior high, long before the buckle bunnies had picked up the chase.

Braden Anderson was all man, and the very definition of rugged, tortured … and beautiful.

Chapter Two

BEAR DIDN'T KNOW what to do with himself as Josie drove away.

He felt—things—and he didn't like it. She'd stirred him up, unsettling his resolve to never feel anything again. He hated feelings. He hated emotional turmoil. Emotions were the one thing he couldn't handle. Emotions were within, and that was where he was weak.

In the hall, Bear pushed himself in a circle to the right, and then to the left, angry and restless and trapped. *Trapped.*

It was bad enough being stuck in this chair, but stuck in this house, the house he'd built for Savannah? It was torture, and because this land was family land, passed to him from his maternal grandfather, Bear was loathe to just sell the place. The house was a prison, but the land meant something to him.

Why hadn't he realized he'd be unhappy here? This enormous house reminded him of a stage set—cold and artificial, and empty. All it did was remind him of how empty his life was and how hollow everything had been for years, and he hadn't even known it. He hadn't realized that nothing in his life had truly been real. Not his strength. Not his career. Not his relationship.

Certainly not his faith.

Bear stopped circling the hall and rolled into the living room with the soaring ceiling and majestic stone fireplace. He went to the wall of windows and stared out across the land that was his, land that he hadn't ever worked, land that was leased to neighbors for their cattle and crops.

His plan had always been to retire and come here to become a rancher just like his grandfather, but it hadn't turned out like that.

He was doing his best to pivot, to focus on his new goals, but living here didn't help. He was far from everything, and nowhere close to the business districts he needed. And if he poured money into renovating this house, it would mean less cash for his new venture, and his venture was his only blue sky. His new venture gave him hope. Purpose. That was what he needed, not a fancy toilet.

Maybe the mistake was to focus on the house. Maybe he just needed to double down on establishing the rehab centers and put on blinders to everything else. The bathroom was difficult, but he managed. The kitchen was a challenge, but he was good with challenges. He just needed to get the right attitude. He needed to prioritize what was important and his comfort wasn't important. Getting the first center opened was the important thing.

Bear rolled back to the entry where Josie had left her business card. In the foyer he drew his phone out of the small pack attached to the chair behind his knees and drew out his phone. He flipped the business card in his fingers, his thumb stroking the matte finish of the thick cream cardstock with the gray-blue ink. *Josie Calhoun, Design Intern.*

Intern.

He shook his head and he exhaled, releasing the bottled air, glad to have come to a decision he could live with.

Quickly he texted her. *Josie, this is Bear Anderson. Thanks for coming out to my place, and I appreciate your input but I'm going a different direction. Sorry to have wasted your time today.*

"WELL?" NEIL ASKED, gesturing Josie into his office as she returned to the company's headquarters in downtown Bozeman. The design practice took up the top two floors of one of the oldest buildings in historic Bozeman. Bookkeeping and support were on the lower floor while the design team had the airy and architectural loft. "How did it go?"

Josie nodded and smiled at Melissa, the other cofounder of the firm who currently sat perched on the edge of a sixties inspired chair, a handful of brochures in her hand.

"I did a brief walk through with him and took notes on what needed to be done."

"What's his budget?" Melissa asked.

Josie lifted a shoulder. "We didn't get that far."

Melissa frowned. "What does he want done?"

"He needs a bathroom and a kitchen that works for him.

I think the kitchen can be modified fairly easily. The bathroom might require tearing down a wall and shifting plumbing."

"How is he getting upstairs to his bedroom?" Neil leaned forward and drew a printed layout of the Anderson house toward him. "All bedrooms are upstairs."

"He's using the downstairs bedroom."

"There is no downstairs bedroom. Just his office which was really a trophy room."

"I didn't see any trophies." Josie approached the desk and leaned over the condensed blueprint of the house. She studied it a moment and then tapped the bedroom with the adjoining bath. "He's sleeping here."

"That was originally his office," Melissa said, leaning over to get a better look at the blueprint, too.

"There wasn't a desk or shelves or trophies," Josie answered. "Just a bed and a nightstand."

"No shelves or cabinets?" Neil persisted.

She shook her head, remembering the plain stark walls. "Nothing."

Neil opened his laptop and typed away and then turned his computer around so Melissa and Josie could see the screen. "This is how that room used to look. It was his favorite room."

Melissa's lips pursed. "I don't think it was his favorite room, but it was his mom's favorite. Or he'd dedicated his wins and success to his mom. Something like that. She'd always been so proud of him, and so he put together the trophy case in her memory and framed some of the articles written about him. I was there one day when the *Rocky Mountain Design Magazine* was doing the feature on his property and the writer was asking Braden about the trophies. I distinctly recall Braden being embarrassed, saying he didn't want to be photographed in that room. In fact, he preferred the room not being included in the magazine feature."

"So, they didn't include it?" Josie asked.

Neil grimaced. "Oh, they did, when the photographer returned to the house for a few shots that the editors still wanted."

"The trophy room photo went into the magazine?" Josie guessed.

"Yes," Neil and Melissa said simultaneously.

"Braden was livid." Melissa glanced at Neil. "I think he's been angry with us ever since then."

"But you couldn't control what the magazine did," Josie protested.

"No. Well, maybe." Neil hesitated. "The fact is, we didn't ask the magazine not to include the trophy room. In hindsight, we probably could have ensured that they didn't. But we didn't think it was that big of a deal."

"No one thought Braden would be hurt," Melissa added quickly, almost defensively. "And it was gorgeous. The most beautiful cabinetry you've ever seen."

Josie just remembered the room as it looked now. Empty, terribly empty, no beautiful cabinetry, no art, nothing decorative anywhere. "I wonder what he did with his trophies and awards."

Neil shrugged. "Maybe he had them moved to a room upstairs."

"Or put in storage," Melissa added. "I can't imagine he would want to sleep in a room filled with reminders of the past."

"True," Josie agreed, before saying goodbye and leaving the office to walk the three short blocks to her studio apartment on the second floor of another old building downtown. Downstairs was a popular restaurant, which meant that it was often noisy, but the staff was friendly and the bartenders protective and kept an eye out for her, especially in the evenings and weekends. She waved at Josh, one of the afternoon waiters who was working the sidewalk tables.

He nodded and then one of the other waiters, Aiden, whistled to get her attention. "Come in, Josie. Have a drink."

She shook her head and smiled. "I've got so much work to do. Maybe this weekend."

"Or a date this weekend?" Aiden answered, lifting a brow, flashing white teeth and a deep dimple in his cheek.

He was good-looking and close to her age, a student at the university, and full of charm. The girls loved him. He knew it, too.

Josie laughed and shook her head. "Not looking to get my heart broken, Aiden, but thank you."

"I'd never break your heart," Aiden vowed, a hand to his chest.

Josie laughed again and, still shaking her head, disappeared through the door to the upstairs apartments. Aiden was gorgeous but young, way too young, and she wasn't looking for a relationship anyway. She was enrolled full-time at the college and working full-time, which meant there was no time for a social life. Besides, she was too serious for most guys she'd met in Bozeman. They wanted to hang out and have fun and she was trying to change the world, make it a better place for everyone. Which was why Josie had always been that odd Calhoun girl with the weird purple eyes and even weirder family.

The labels didn't bother her anymore. She was who she was, and it didn't matter if she didn't fit in. Maybe she wasn't supposed to fit in but do something important, and if that was the case, then she was doing just fine.

Josie sat down on her thrift store loveseat which she'd recovered herself and pulled her laptop from her bag, preparing to jump on her homework when she spotted a text in Messages on her computer.

Josie, this is Bear Anderson. Thanks for coming out to my place, and I appreciate your input but I'm going a different direction. Sorry to have wasted your time today.

Josie sighed, not entirely surprised by his decision, but disappointed nonetheless. She'd wanted to work with him—

not just because Bear needed help—but she'd been excited by the project, one which would have fulfilled the requirements for her program.

She was getting so close to being out of school and finally being able to pursue the jobs that interested her, rather than the ones Neil and Melissa assigned her.

But she'd made it this far. She'd find a way to fulfill her program requirements without Bear. She just needed to focus and spread the word. Perhaps it was time to reach out to some of the senior homes in Park County and see if any of them were open to her donating her services … if they could pay for the materials.

Josie put away her phone without rereading Bear's message, but it stayed with her, and it gave her a prickly feeling in her middle. Excitement and nerves and a tingly awareness that couldn't possibly be attraction.

She'd only just met him, too. Worse, she hadn't been attracted to anyone in years. What was it about him?

It couldn't be his beautiful face. Or those massive shoulders. Or the tan muscular forearms.

No, she wasn't that shallow.

Her attraction went deeper. She was drawn to something internal, a toughness that came with battle scars. She shouldn't be drawn to scars—real or imaginary—but Josie didn't always do the expected thing. She had a long history of doing what everyone thought she shouldn't do.

Maybe Bear going a different direction with his house

was a blessing in disguise. But first—before she moved on—there was something she had to do. Whether he liked it or not.

She called her brother Rye, hoping he'd be free to pick up, and he did.

"What's up, Jo?" he asked, answering.

"Rye, I need a favor, and it's a big one."

"Are you in trouble?"

"No. No, it's a work thing, and I'm trying to pull off a miracle, and you're the only one who can make it happen."

"I'm not particularly good with miracles, Josie, especially this time of year. I'm slammed."

"I know. And I wouldn't ask if I didn't really need you."

"Can it wait a couple weeks?"

"No."

"Josie, this is when I make my money."

"I know, but it's important, Rye. Trust me."

"I do trust you, but I've promised the Gradys we'd be finished with their kitchen by the weekend."

"Haven't they changed their mind on the layout three times? Different stone, different stove, different windows? And didn't they expect you to absorb the cost for the mistake she made with the stone?"

Rye exhaled on a growl. "So, what's the emergency? Did you break something?"

"No, but you will be. I need you to widen a door. Fortunately, it's an interior door and I was hoping you could swap the interior door for one that's wider."

Rye sighed. "So where am I going?"

"Clyde Park. A property off Brackett Creek Road."

"Are you being deliberately vague?"

"You're going to Braden Anderson's home. I need you to widen his bathroom door. And replace his ramp with something more custom. If you can."

"I thought your firm was fired."

"They were, yes, but if you saw his ramp—its shiny metal, and it's an eyesore, and it looks institutional."

Rye remained silent and Josie's pulse quickened, fueled by determination. "Nothing works for him, Rye. He can't use his kitchen. He struggles to use his bathroom. He's all boxed in. And I'm not asking you to fix all of that. Just give him a bigger bathroom door and I'll feel better. He will, too."

"You've met him?"

"I have. Today. And he's … struggling. I wouldn't call him angry, but he's frustrated and when you see what he's dealing with, you'll understand why. I think having a slightly more functional bathroom would make him feel better. And replacing the metal ramp with something else—"

"The ramp is going to have to wait, sis. I can go and measure the bathroom and make some calls and see if Paradise Lumber has something in stock, and if they do, I can get this done tomorrow. But the ramp will be later, once we've caught up on my contracted jobs."

"That's great. I'll call Paradise Lumber and see if they have anything that would work."

"Let me know what you find out."

"I will."

Chapter Three

BEAR WOKE UP in a cold sweat, the sheet tangled around his hips and legs, his upper body thrashing.

He didn't know what he'd dreamed but it had made his heart race, and his breathing was still ragged as he tried to orient himself. This was his room. This was his Clyde Park ranch house. This was home.

Or it was supposed to be his home.

Unfortunately, there was little of him here, little of who he'd been, little of who he'd become.

If anything, this house was a haunting reminder of what had happened to him. Once he could do anything, and he'd done everything, and nothing stopped him. But that person was gone. Forever.

It crossed Bear's mind that he should start therapy again. Everyone who knew him thought it was a good idea, but after years of counseling, he was sick of talking, sick of peeling back the pain, sick of trying to explain the fury and helplessness of being broken.

He was not made to be helpless. Worse, his helplessness was accentuated here in this house. He struggled doing every little thing from sleeping to eating to peeing to bathing.

He slammed into corners and walls. He fell transferring to the shower chair. He fell transferring back to his chair from the toilet.

He fell sideways, and then fell forward and fell back, and if he was lucky, there was something for him to grab and use as leverage. But sometimes, there was nothing, and he crawled to his chair and then it took every bit of his upper body strength to lift up off the ground. And, eventually, he did get back in the chair. But sometimes it took a while. And sometimes it took longer than that, but that was because he was probably pounding his fist into the ground, into his leg, into the cushion of his chair, pounding and swearing and breaking things, including himself.

This was not the life for him. This was not his future. This shouldn't be his house.

He should have said as much to beautiful lavender-eyed Josie Calhoun with her dark hair and full mouth and questions. So many questions, and she wasn't wrong to ask them, and her feedback hadn't been wrong, either. If anything, her feedback was spot on. She knew what she was talking about. She knew what would make his life easier here. She knew the changes that needed to be made.

But, good Lord, she was too pretty. Too pretty, too determined, too optimistic.

If she was around him long enough, she'd see the real Bear. The one that suffered and struggled, and how there were days he couldn't handle the suffering and struggling.

How there were days he just hurt all over. And there were days he couldn't get the catheter in and there were days he had infections that made him need a trip to ER because his fever had spiked, and he'd waited too long to get on antibiotics.

But how did he know he needed an antibiotic when he couldn't feel his bladder? Or his lower body? Or half of his back?

That was why he'd told her to stay away. He functioned best when no one was close. He didn't have to be afraid of being seen for who he really was.

Not necessarily broken but changed. And sometimes so confused. There were days he was fine with it, and then there were days he didn't know how to cope.

The therapists said it was normal. The doctors said it would take time—years—to adjust. But Bear had already prided himself on his control. On his ability to tolerate pain and overcome what most cowboys couldn't.

But he wasn't that man anymore.

He was a man with rage and moods and darkness, and he couldn't let this darkness out. He couldn't let anyone know or see, much less pretty Josie Calhoun with her sunny self-assurance and the dimple deep in her cheek.

The last thing he wanted to do was hurt her. Crush her. God knew the world needed more optimism. He craved her optimism. Today, she'd exuded light and hope. She'd felt like pure oxygen.

But he remembered his last attempt at a relationship. He remembered the nurse he'd dated for four months last autumn. She'd been sweet and hopeful, too, and he'd crushed her. She'd been a little bit older than Josie, but she was similar in her kindness and determination to help. She'd been certain she could make things better.

But no one could make things right—short of God reaching down and healing his spine, and that wasn't going to happen. He wasn't going to walk. He wasn't going to run. He wasn't going to kneel. And he wasn't going to be making love.

Who he was, what he was, would never be the same.

Bear struggled to sit up, and bracing his upper body with one arm, he yanked the damp tangled sheet out from his legs and gave it a little toss, cooling his skin, smoothing the sheet. He did it again, this time to calm his thoughts. Whatever he'd dreamed had upset him, and it was time to pull himself together.

He wasn't going to slip into self-pity or despair. He couldn't go to such a dark place, not again. He'd been there before, and it had been a battle to claw himself up, and out. He'd never understood depression until Savannah was gone and his world was narrow, reduced to appointment after appointment, just to regain control over his body.

He had control now. It wasn't perfect, and he wasn't perfect, but he was better than he'd been two and a half years ago. Heck, the doctors hadn't even thought he'd survive the accident, never mind come out of the coma. He'd been in the coma for almost a month, and there was concern he'd be brain damaged, along with paralyzed.

Thank God, he'd been saved from that, and he had independence now—hard won. Bear was proud of the strides he'd made, proud that despite his terrible fears, he'd moved forward, and he was doing something positive again. Something that wasn't just about himself.

Maybe he had too many scars and legs that didn't work but he had his brain, and his spirit wasn't broken, and he was going to keep fighting—not just for himself but all the others with spinal cord injuries who needed someone in their corner. Bear was going to be in their corner. Bear was going to make sure others didn't have to struggle alone.

Bear's chest burned, and his eyes felt gritty. He blinked and swallowed around the ache in his throat, and the ache in his heart.

Thirty-three months ago, he couldn't stop asking why.

Thank goodness, he'd finally reached the point where he could say, *why not?*

BEAR WAS OUTSIDE retrieving his wallet from his Bronco when a blue truck appeared in his driveway and parked not far from where Bear was waiting.

A man wearing a trucker hat climbed out of his vehicle

and came forward, hand extended. "Rye Calhoun," he said introducing himself before looking at the ramp behind Bear. "That is an eyesore of a ramp. I'm sorry."

Bear glanced from the ramp, not quite as offensively shiny in the early morning light, to the man in the trucker hat. "Can I help you?"

"I think I'm here to help you." The stranger settled his trucker hat more firmly on his head, his dark hair long at the back, brushing the collar of his shirt. "I'm with Calhoun Construction."

That still didn't resonate with Bear. "Sent by whom? The design firm?"

"No. My sister. Josie."

Bear was beginning to understand. "I told her Tuesday I didn't need her help."

Rye rocked back on his heels, hands on his hips. "She said it was an emergency."

Bear shook his head. "No emergency. Just ticked off that I'm destroying my house with my chair."

"I have a bigger interior door in the back of the truck for your bathroom. I'd hoped to get here yesterday but Paradise Lumber needed a day to track down a wider door for me. But I've got it now and it won't take long for me to swap it out."

"How do you know that your door would work?"

"Doors come in standard sizes, and Josie thought you had a thirty inch bathroom door. The one in my truck is thirty-six inches. If that's the case it'd give you a lot more room."

The corner of Bear's mouth lifted. "I don't suppose you happen to have a bigger bathroom in that flatbed? As Josie might have told you, mine is pretty small."

"I heard. Why don't you show me?"

"No need. I'm making do, and I hate to waste your time—"

"I'm already here. At least seeing your problem bathroom would make me feel better."

"You're sounding just as stubborn as your sister."

Rye's eyes glinted. "Oh, she's worse than me. But then, she's a far better human. Josie will give the shirt off her back while I prefer to keep mine on."

Bear was torn between exasperation and amusement. "I haven't had coffee yet and I'm feeling it. You're welcome to come in but know that I'm not planning on putting any money into this house, not when I've decided it doesn't work for me."

"You're going to sell it?"

"I don't know if I will sell or just lease it. But it isn't comfortable and making the changes your sister suggested—" Bear broke off, jaw tightening. "I know how those projects are. One thing leads to another and another and it ends up taking months and twice the amount of money budgeted."

"Or three times."

"Exactly."

"But you should rest assured that Josie is quite thrifty and is more sensitive to finances than many. We grew up without much, and she learned to create beauty out of thrift stores and hand-me-downs.

"I don't doubt it, but remodels are exhausting, and I don't have it in me."

"Completely respect that." Rye approached the ramp but instead of walking up it, he climbed the wide porch's partially obscured front steps as he studied the ramp's design. "Why didn't they put the ramp off to the side?" he asked, taking another stair. "There's plenty of space in your yard and you wouldn't have had to destroy the symmetry of your front entrance."

"Would it have worked there?"

"Absolutely." Rye pointed to the rustic railing on one side. "That would have been a perfect place for the ramp to go. You'd only have had to remove those five-foot pieces, and you'd have had a great landing with minimal damage to the structure. It's still just as close to the front door, but it provides a better area to arrive, with more room to turn."

Bear rolled back slightly to study the side of the front porch. Rye was right. "How come you can see that so quickly and others can't?"

"We've had years to learn what works for a wheelchair and what doesn't. Not sure if Josie told you, but our younger brother Jasper has cerebral palsy and is in an electric chair. His chair, by necessity, is big and bulky, so space is always at a premium."

"She probably mentioned it, but I was in a terrible mood, and missed half of what she said. I owe her an apology."

"It couldn't have upset her that much. She still called and asked me to help you."

"She shouldn't have."

"No, probably not, but Josie's not your average bear—no pun intended."

Bear reluctantly smiled. "Come in, check out the bathroom, and I'll meet you in the kitchen." He turned and with a push of his right hand, moved into the house with Rye following. "When I turn left into the kitchen, you just keep going down the hall and the first door on the right is my bedroom and bathroom. Ignore the mess if you can. I wasn't expecting visitors."

Bear filled his mug with coffee and waited for Rye to reappear. Rye was gone longer than Bear had expected.

"Wasn't sure if you were working or just needed to use the facilities," Bear said when Rye finally appeared.

Rye laughed. "Today it was just lots of note taking."

"With what?"

"My phone." He pulled the phone out of his back pocket. "I dictate everything these days, makes it much easier than trying to scribble it down." Rye nodded at the coffee pot. "If you have coffee to spare, I'd love a cup."

Bear scooted to the edge of his seat and stretched an arm

up to retrieve a mug. "Creamer is in the fridge, if you want it."

Rye took the carton of creamer out and topped off his coffee before putting the creamer back. "You definitely need the bigger bathroom door. You're destroying the one that's there now."

"It's a tight fit getting the chair in there, which is why I think I'm better off just finding a place that will work for me—a place that has everything I need already, without having to take on a renovation job."

"I'm not sure there are going to be a lot of places like that around here. You might have to move into Bozeman. With a city you'd have more options."

"I'm not a city guy. I've been on the outskirts of Nashville for a number of years, and I moved back to Montana wanting a different quality of life."

"You'll get that here." Rye's tone was ironic. "There aren't a lot of people out this way."

"I have found it rather remote."

"Did your girl move back with you?"

Bear shook his head. "No. I moved back on my own. And there is no girl," he smiled grimly. "Or woman. Just me."

"This house is certainly big for one person."

"It's big for two people. I only use a couple rooms here. No point hanging onto it, not when someone else could enjoy it. I certainly don't enjoy it."

"Would you enjoy it more if it were accessible? Put in an elevator, get those necessary changes to your master bedroom and bathroom."

"No. I built this for my fiancé. We made a lot of decisions together. I wanted the great room's wall of windows and the wood—the hundred-year-old barn beams and flooring. She was all about size and the finishes, bigger, better, more luxurious. So, it has both of us here. I'm the timber and rustic wood. Savannah's the expensive finishes and additional six thousand feet no one needs."

"But you agreed to her ideas."

"I figured we would have a lot of kids. I always wanted a lot of kids. But that's not going to happen a now, and this place just reminds me of a time, and a life, that no longer exists."

"You have to get out of here in that case. I wouldn't stay either." Rye sipped his coffee. "But if you are hoping to lease this place, or one day sell it, you'll want to make a few repairs. I'm not suggesting I need to do the work. In fact, I'm pretty slammed during the summer months, but that bathroom of yours and the bedroom have seen better days. The walls and doors are scuffed, and there's a place the drywall looks like something hit it—"

"Me."

Rye grinned. "I wasn't going to say it. But once you get the new bathroom door in, I can recommend some painters and they can come in and do the necessary touch ups." He hesitated. "If you're tempted to stay, I'd suggest replacing the vanity and the shower, making it a roll-in shower. But if you're serious about leaving, don't spend the money. Just give it a refresh so it doesn't look like your walls and cabinets have been feuding with your chair."

"Oh, they have. My casters make contact with virtually everything, every day."

"Our old house up in Eureka was the same. Between my dad's chair and my brothers chair—"

"Your dad's in a chair?"

"He had a roofing accident. Broke his back. Happened about ten years ago."

"That's rough."

"It is what it is."

"No wonder your sister said she's passionate about accessible design."

"My dad's accident was hard on her … hard on all of us, but especially her. She'd always been a daddy's girl and seeing him so changed turned her into a warrior, determined to make things better—for as many people as she can."

"She's certainly something."

"Josie can be a lot," Rye said ruefully.

"That's not what I meant. Your sister is…" Bear hesitated. "She's young. And confident." *And ridiculously pretty*, he added silently.

"Ambitious," Rye added. "As well as passionate about design."

"Nashville is full of beautiful ambitious women, but your sister is different."

"Maybe it's because she doesn't have a lot of ego." Rye shrugged. "Hard to be cocky when you're considered the poor family in town."

"That bad?"

"After Dad couldn't work, it got pretty grim for a number of years. Happily, we're all doing better now. Moving from Eureka to Park County was a good decision for the entire family."

"There are more of you?"

Rye grinned. "Another sister."

"Is she into design, too?"

"No. Hannah's a nurse and wrapping up her degree in Missoula. We're hoping she'll be moving back once she graduates at the end of the year. My family really misses her, especially Jasper."

"He's the one with CP?"

"He'll be nineteen this year."

"You said he's doing better since you moved?" Bear asked.

"He's working with a physical therapist that's been helping him with his strength and mobility. She's also really pretty, which motivates my brother."

Bear laughed. "Sounds just like the motivation he needs."

Rye gestured. "I just had a thought. Why don't you

make your current bedroom and bathroom suite more accessible, not less? That way when you go to sell the house, you'd have something unique on the market. It's hard to find a home that is accessible for different needs, and if your downstairs suite could accommodate someone like my brother Jasper, or others who can't manage stairs, you'd be helping people out. Lots of families want a ground floor suite for their parents or in-laws. And should you decide not to sell the house, you have a space that works for you."

"Your sister suggested the same thing, but I don't want to invest more in this house. I'm not ready to sell it, but I'm also unwilling to put more money into it." He glanced down into his coffee before looking up at Rye. "I would appreciate you giving me a bid for replacing the bathroom door and basic touchups and repairs—like covering up the hole from my fist in the wall."

"Do you have any objection to me including Josie? She could use the work. She has to put together a portfolio to graduate." Rye quickly added, "Best of all, she's very affordable. She's free right now. At least until she graduates."

"That would be taking advantage of her."

"No. Trust me. You'd be doing her a favor."

Bear studied Rye a moment. "You're protective of her."

"We're close. Adversity breaks some people, while it brings others together. For us—Josie, Hannah, and me—the challenges just made us grow closer."

"You're lucky."

Rye's head inclined. "I am."

RYE PHONED JOSIE as he left Bear's ranch.

"How did it go? Any problem getting the door in?" she asked.

"He didn't know I was coming."

"Was that a problem?"

Rye sighed. "Josie."

"So, tell me what happened."

"The door is still in the back of my truck."

"Oh no!"

"He's decided he doesn't want to stay in the house. He's going to start looking for a place that would already be accessible."

"But he can't sell the house with that bathroom looking like a teenager took a bat to it."

"I don't think he used a bat, but he's agreed to get the damage fixed."

"Seems as if you got along much better with him than I did. Everything I said annoyed him."

"I don't think that's the case. He seemed impressed by you."

"No."

"He did say he owes you an apology—"

"He doesn't," she answered quickly.

"If he thinks he does, he does. Men usually know when they've crossed the line." Rye merged onto the frontage road, easing between a huge semi-truck hauling lumber and another truck hauling livestock.

"I didn't think he crossed a line. I think he was just frustrated with his situation and unwilling to invest a lot more into a house that wasn't making him happy. It's a shame, though, as it's a gorgeous place—at least what I saw of it."

"He does have an incredible view of the Crazies."

"It was his grandfather's property, which is why I'd hate to see him sell it."

"But the house was built for his fiancé, and that weighs on him."

"That's a problem," she agreed.

"I gave him the name of the realtor I used when Ansley and I bought our house in Marietta. Not sure if Bear needs one, but Paul was honest and easy to work with."

"Thank you for taking the time to go out there. I really appreciate it, Rye."

"I know you do, and I'm glad I went. Bear's a good guy. I liked him, and happy to help him out."

Chapter Four

THE WEEK PASSED quickly with Josie spending every free hour at her desk, putting the finishing details on a proposal Melissa asked her to work on. The project was a big one and would bring in significant income and recognition to the firm, but first they needed to get the job. A number of other design firms were putting in proposals, too, for the new private club with luxury homes that would be built in Gardiner, just outside Yellowstone. Melissa had done a considerable amount of work but wanted Josie to polish up the power point presentation, along with ensuring that their proposal included universal design elements.

Josie had been more than happy to review and polish, feeling strongly that public—and private—spaces should be flexible and inclusive. People changed. People aged. Homes and community spaces should grow with people.

It was easy for her to get lost in the work, and it wasn't until her alarm buzzed, letting her know it was time to leave for class, that she realized just how focused she'd been. Hours had gone by, and she hadn't even had lunch and now there would be no time.

She quickly changed, grabbed her backpack, and headed

down the stairs to Main Street when she spotted someone bumping across the street in a wheelchair. She recognized the wide set of the shoulders and the square jaw.

What was Bear Anderson doing in Bozeman?

Josie hurried across the street and caught up with him before he reached the next light.

She tapped him on the shoulder. "Hey," she said, suddenly nervous as he turned to face her. "Hi. It's Josie."

The edge of his mouth lifted. "I know who you are."

"How are you?"

"Good. And you?"

"Very good. Just off to class." She glanced around. "What are you doing in Bozeman?"

"I'm meeting with a commercial real estate agent. He's going to show me a few available spaces for a business I'm starting."

"That's exciting. But what about your home? Are you staying or looking for something different? Rye said you might want to move."

"I'm only looking to rent a place for now, but yes, that's on my to-do list, too."

Josie glanced at her watch. She was going to be late for class for sure. "I need to go, but if you ever need anything—even mediocre design ideas," she said with a wink, "you've got my card."

His eyes crinkled as he smiled. "I do."

BEAR DID CALL Josie that evening. "I wanted to apologize for being rude when you arrived at my house. I was an ass, and I'm sorry. I hope you can forgive me."

"I already have."

He cleared his throat. "You can't make it that easy."

"Of course I can. I appreciate the apology but we're all human and we all make mistakes."

"I wasn't angry with you—"

"I know."

"Or the design firm. I was angry with myself."

"Why angry with yourself?"

"The house isn't mine."

"I don't understand. I thought you built it."

Bear didn't know how to explain, and with anyone else, wouldn't.

But he wanted to try telling her. "I did, but I built the house for my fiancé, Savannah. We were planning our wedding, and I was building our future family home. There is a lot of her here—every place I look, I see her—and it's not comfortable. It's not where I want to be. Even if it was accessible, it's not my home, not anymore."

"That makes sense."

"You'd think I would have known that when I made plans to return to Montana, but I didn't. It took me some time to get to this realization. I'd thought being trapped downstairs was the issue, but as time went on, I realized there was more to it. This house wasn't good for me. I wasn't good. I wasn't coping well."

"But now you know. So you can do something about it."

"Are you always so positive?"

"I like to be," she said. "If I've learned anything in life is that while we can't control what's happened, we can hopefully control how we respond to what's going on now."

"Your family has had more than its fair share of challenges."

"I think that's a fair assessment, but it's also brought us closer. Hannah, Rye, and I make a formidable team."

"Your brother said the same thing."

"See? We're pretty tight."

"I'm going to be hiring Rye's crew to fix my bathroom, but I've also let him know that if I find a place for my business, I'd like him to do any work needed. He suggested I talk to you about my business plans and see if what I'm doing could work for your design project required for graduation."

"I'm interested."

He laughed. "Wait. I'm supposed to sell you on the idea."

"You can still do that."

"Good, as I'm going to see commercial properties in Bozeman Saturday morning, and I wondered if I could meet you for lunch after? I'll fill you in then, if that would work for you."

"That's great. I have no plans for Saturday. Just tell me when and where."

"I don't know Bozeman well," he said. "Can you recommend a place?"

"I'll send you some names. Look at the menus, and we can do whatever sounds best to you."

"I want you to enjoy it, too."

"Oh, I will," she teased. "I'm only recommending restaurants I like."

They said goodbye and twenty minutes later Bear got a text from Josie.

Every place on this list has great food and is wheelchair friendly. I've eaten at several of them with my family. Most take reservations. The Copper Kid is the only one that doesn't.

Bear skimmed the list before checking out each of the links. The menus looked good, and equally accessible, which was a plus in a town with historic buildings. In the end, he chose the restaurant with a pretty shaded patio, requesting a table for two on the patio at one o'clock. With the reservation confirmed, he texted Josie back with the restaurant and the time of their reservation.

She liked his text and then answered. *Looking forward to it.*

For the first time in a long time, Bear almost smiled. He was looking forward to lunch, too. And seeing Josie. She was the draw, not the meal, but his attraction to her unsettled him for the same reasons she'd unsettled him last week. She was too pretty, too young, too optimistic … for him the way he was now. It wasn't that he couldn't appreciate a beautiful woman, but he couldn't get tangled up … or tangle her, either.

BEAR SAW FOUR different properties Saturday morning and none of them were quite right for him. The building would need a big parking lot, and it needed to be conveniently located next to the building, not across the street or down the street, or in a parking tower. The building itself needed to be open and spacious, with lots of interior room for equipment and wheelchairs, which ruled out most of the turn of the century buildings downtown, and close to it. The building shouldn't have a lot of windows—his clientele wanted privacy—but he hoped to put in sky lights to create an abundance of natural lighting. There was nothing worse than being cooped up in a building with just harsh strips of flourescents overhead.

Bear had a vision, a very clear vision of the business he wanted, and how the space would look and function, but nothing he saw today worked, and he wasn't going to compromise on what he wanted. He'd just have to keep looking.

He was the first to reach the restaurant and the hostess seated him at the table on the patio, beneath a big umbrella and the shade of adjacent trees. It was warm without being hot, and the breeze rustled the leaves above, making it a perfect day for lunch outside.

A waitress led Josie to the table a few minutes later. Flushed and smiling, Josie greeted him breathlessly. "Am I late?"

"No. I just arrived," he said, rolling back and drawing out her chair for her.

"Oh, good." She sat down and gave him a brilliant smile, a smile that lit her eyes and made her teeth flash.

The waitress asked what they wanted to drink and disappeared.

Josie leaned toward Bear. "So? How did it go? Success?"

He shook his head. "Not great, but I'm not giving up. It's just a matter of time."

"What are you looking for? Maybe I can help you," she asked, her violet gaze meeting his. "I'm good at finding things. Just ask Melissa and Neil at the firm."

Her smile burrowed into his chest, catching his breath and Bear shifted uncomfortably. What was it about her that unsettled him so much? Women never made him uncomfortable before. But Josie ... she was different. And he'd changed. He was different now. Not a good different; not the kind of different where he could offer her more. He would only ever be able to offer her less.

But this wasn't a date, he reminded himself. This was business. "I welcome any and all help. My commercial real estate agent is running out of options for me in Bozeman. Now something could come on the market in the coming months, but I don't want to wait months to get started. I'm ready to get going now."

"Are you locked into Bozeman, or are there any other areas you're interested in? What are your requirements in terms of square footage and other essentials?"

"Let me tell you a little about my business first, which should help explain my requirements as I have specific needs as my clientele have specific needs."

She pulled out her phone. "Can I make notes?"

"Of course, and to answer your question, no, I'm not locked into Bozeman. It is the biggest city in the area and seemed like the best place for my first location. However, there's no reason I can't open a location elsewhere first."

She looked at him. "What do you want to do?"

"I'm interested in opening a facility where those with SCI—"

"Spinal cord injury?"

He nodded. "Yes. At my facility, people could come and take advantage of a robotic walker for a half day, or day—after training how to use it. Just this year, Medicaid agreed to start covering exoskeletons for personal home use—but not very many have been approved yet and even then, the patient is still out the deductible, which is about twenty percent."

"Are these exoskeletons terribly expensive?'

"About one hundred thousand dollars each."

"Wow," she whispered.

"Over time the cost will come down a little, but not enough for most people. Which is why I want to create facilities where those who would greatly benefit from using one, could have access to them without bankrupting them. The intent is that folks could make a reservation and come use one, just like one would for a personal trainer or a spa appointment."

"Have you used one before?"

"I actually own one of my own. I haven't used it recently but should. They're not sufficient exercise for me to consider them a workout, but they're good for everything else. It's important those with SCI get up and stand. It helps with circulation, reduces infections, sores, everything."

"I've never heard very much about them. How were you introduced to them? At a rehab facility?"

"I've been involved with the technology for years, long before I was hurt. I became interested in exoskeletons when my friend Sean O'Leary was paralyzed in an accident. I, like everyone on the circuit, am aware of the dangers. Every year, someone dies in this sport, whether it's a high school kid, college kid, or a professional. It's dangerous. Just like motocross is dangerous, and other extreme sports. But it's different when it's someone close to you that is hurt, you know?"

She nodded but didn't interrupt him.

After a moment, he continued. "I wanted to be there for

Sean. I wanted to know as much as I could, and I did a lot of reading, and a lot of research, and I discovered one of the most important things is getting someone with spinal cord injury on their feet. It helps address a large number of health issues and complications. Someone put me in touch with Dylan Sheenan—he's from Paradise Valley, comes from an old ranching family—now working in high tech in Austin. He's taken his success and become an investor in robotics—"

"Robotics?"

"Exoskeletons are a form of robotics, and robotics can help those with spinal cord injuries potentially walk again and regain some movement. It's still a new field. Every major university hospital is working on trials, but they're not readily available in communities."

"If they're that important to one's quality of life, why have you stopped using yours?" she asked.

"I've just been busy, and its time consuming getting it on."

"But you have to make the time, Bear. I mean, if you believe in it so much."

He smiled crookedly. "You make excellent points. But when you see what one looks like, you'll understand why having a clinic where someone can go to get assistance matters so much to me. No one with an injury wants to be a burden on his or her family, and this way, there is a place they can go to get support from those who understand what they're going through."

"I'm impressed. This sounds very exciting and futuristic. I keep thinking of the Iron Man from Avengers, you know how Robert Downey Jr's character had that external suit he wore which allowed him to be stronger, faster and do those extraordinary stunts?"

"You might want to temper those expectations then. The existing exoskeleton designs are practical, but not stylish. They definitely don't have all those bells and whistles, but maybe someday." Amusement lightened his expression. "Maybe someday there will be a robotic suit that would allow someone with a spinal cord injury gain more freedom—not just walking and climbing a few stairs but running. Hiking. Being more fully active. I like to think it's possible. I would love to think it's possible in my lifetime, but what we have now is better than nothing. What we have now is promising."

"But not accessible for most."

"Exactly."

"And that's your goal."

"Yes."

YES. HIS ANSWER, so firm, so determined, resonated with her. Their eyes locked, held, and something in Bear's gaze made Josie go warm, and the heat spread through her, starting in her chest, seeping into her middle, her arms and legs.

It felt good to understand what was driving him. It felt even better to feel enthusiastic about his goal. She saw his vision and believed in it. Her work wasn't so dissimilar from his.

Suddenly, she was reminded of his friend Sean, which was how Bear had gotten involved in robotics in the first place. "What about Sean?" she asked. "Has he also embraced the exoskeleton? Did it make a difference for him?"

Bear's expression changed. He glanced away, his voice deepening. "It didn't."

The husky note in his voice was pain, and Josie realized she'd wandered into a sensitive area, and it was better to leave the subject alone.

She took a sip from her water glass before speaking. "I think you're on to something, and if anyone could make it happen, it would be you."

He looked back at her, some of his tension easing. "Why me?"

"Because you're Bear Anderson. Montana legend." Her smile wavered, and she bit down on the inside of her cheek to keep her emotions in check.

Somehow, in just a few conversations, Bear had gotten under her skin. She was drawn to him, and it wasn't pity that made her respond to him, but something far more powerful. It felt destined somehow. It felt as if she was supposed to know him, and as if they were supposed to work together.

"So, at the same time you're looking for a spot for your business, you're also looking for a new home?" she asked.

"I know. It's a lot. I'm hoping to find a place I can rent soon and then I'll work on leasing my ranch."

"I'm glad you're not going to sell it."

"I don't think I could, not right now. I have a lot of great memories of visiting my grandparents there, and spending summers helping my granddad out. He's the one that got me interested in riding and roping."

"And bull riding?"

Bear grimaced. "No, he wasn't a fan of bull riding. He thought it was for showoffs."

She smiled. "Is it?"

"Yes."

Josie laughed.

His smile faded. "I wish I hadn't torn down my grandparents' house. I wish I'd left it standing and built the new house somewhere else. There is plenty of land. It would have been a far better use of my money—and it could have been a good home for me now."

"But you didn't because of the view," she guessed.

He nodded.

"Down the road, should you want to return to your ranch, I'm sure you could find another spot with the view that will also give you privacy from your neighbors."

"I don't have any close neighbors."

"But you would, if you sold your big house." She hesitated. "The other thing you might consider is leasing the house for now, and then one day—again, down the road—using the house as part of a family compound. You'd have a new, different house that met your needs, and that big log cabin could become the gathering spot for your kids and their families."

"I can't have kids."

She shrugged. "What about your sister? Does she have kids?"

"A whole pack of them."

"So, there you go. When your sister visits, she and her pack can stay in the big house, and you'll have your house, and everyone will create new memories and traditions."

He studied her a moment, a hint of humor in his silver-gray eyes. "It's an interesting idea."

"I'm full of ideas," she agreed. "Hopefully now and then, I have a good one."

"I do think you're on to something, though. Perhaps I could lease the house out for a couple of years and once my business is a go, I can decide what's right for me. Right now, I just want something that's smaller. I'm lost in the big house."

"And possibly more comfortable?" She flashed, unable to hide her smile.

"That would be nice. It'd be great not to fall out of my wheelchair quite so often."

Her eyes widened. "Does that happen often?"

"Only in the bathroom, but that's about to change."

"Good." She was about to add something when the waitress who'd been hovering in the background for the past ten minutes finally asserted herself and appeared at their table.

"Are you ready to order?" she asked, notepad and pen in hand.

Bear had glanced over the menu before Josie arrived and ordered a bison burger with a green salad. Josie ordered the big summer salad with grilled chicken.

When the waitress left, Josie returned to the subject they were discussing before the interruption. "You didn't ask for my opinion, but I'm going to give it anyway. I think you want to live near where you'll be working. You should cut that commute down. I can't imagine doing a lot of driving every day would be all that good for you."

He shrugged. "I don't mind driving."

"You've been in Tennessee too long. Our winters aren't as nice as Nashville. The icy roads are dangerous, and frequently closed, especially out by you. Find a place close to your business, preferably in town, so you can take meetings and meet people and become part of the community."

"You like Bozeman that much?"

"It's a great university town, with lots to do here with the restaurants and bars and entertainment. But Rye has settled in Marietta, and he really likes it there. Marietta is much smaller than Bozeman, with maybe twelve or thirteen thousand people. But it's not a college town, and it's more small town. It reminds me of Livingston with its old brick buildings and historic downtown." She paused. "You've been to Marietta, right?"

"A few times, mostly to check out the medical center."

"Marietta Medical is impressive, isn't it?

"I mostly drove around the complex. I understand it's grown quite a bit in the past decade."

"Marietta Medical has received significant endowments from several very generous benefactors allowing it to become a state-of-the-art medical facility. They have some of the best doctors in the state."

"I like that."

"My brother Jasper's medical team is in Bozeman and they're really good, but Rye has suggested we switch his care to the specialists at Marietta Medical. They just have a lot of growth and energy."

"Sounds like you favor Marietta."

Josie laughed. "You should talk to Rye. They're on the outskirts of Marietta and they're very happy. They have ten acres because Rye loved his horses, but he's finally retired from the rodeo—at Ansley's insistence. She was afraid he'd be hurt, and we already have two men in my family in wheelchairs. We didn't need him hurt, too." And then Josie realized what she'd said, and to whom she'd said it, and she went hot and cold, immediately ashamed. "That came out wrong," she added quickly. "There's nothing wrong with being in a wheelchair."

"Oh, there's everything wrong with being in a wheelchair," he answered gruffly, "but it's better than being dead."

She closed her eyes, appalled by her thoughtlessness. "I wish the ground would just open up and swallow me whole."

"That might be a tough one to come back from."

"Fair enough." Josie took a quick deep breath. "What else can I tell you about Marietta? It's got a thriving economy and even people new to town—like Rye and Ansley—feel welcome."

"Was your brother in construction before he retired from competing?"

"He was a roofer then, but this year he got his contractor's license and now owns a roofing and construction company. He's really happy."

"And your sister-in-law? Is she at home? Do they have kids?"

"No kids, not yet. Ansley is an artist and has a gallery in downtown Marietta, right on Main Street, and she's doing so well. Rye was worried she wouldn't be able to make her rent every month, but it hasn't been a problem. People love her work, and she loves painting, and it's a win-win."

"What does she paint? Portraits? Landscapes?"

"Landscapes. Big, big canvases, too. Texas, Montana, Idaho, Wyoming. She recently did an exhibit at a prestigious gallery in Jackson Hole and everything sold by the end of the second night. She's already been invited back for next year."

"Impressive."

"She really is. Next time you visit Marietta, check out her gallery, Ansley Art. You might even find something perfect for your new place."

He grinned. "You Calhouns stick together, don't you?"

"Just a little bit."

Chapter Five

Nashville

"MORNING SICKNESS GONE?" Dr. Matthews asked, glancing at Savannah as he rolled forward on his low stool to approach where she lay, stomach bared, on the examination table.

Savannah Webb nodded. "Never had it bad, but the nausea's definitely gone" she said, flinching as he placed the chilly fetal Doppler on her belly.

Instinctively, she held her breath as her obstetrician moved the flat cold ultrasound around, placing the wand in different spots on her flat stomach to get the best position to listen to the heartbeat.

She didn't want to hear the heartbeat. Didn't want to think of the baby. Didn't want a baby. But here she was, having another checkup, trying to buy time and figure out what to do when time was the very thing she couldn't buy … not if she was going to end the pregnancy.

She should just end the pregnancy.

"Sounds good," Dr. Matthews said, lifting the Doppler and giving her an encouraging smile. "Nice strong heartbeat."

She didn't smile back. She couldn't speak. She'd vowed she'd never do this again, go through this again. And yet here she was. Pregnant. *Again.*

She'd ended the pregnancy last time. That decision, two years ago, had been brutal. It tore her up, haunting her. She'd vowed then, never to go that route again. But here she was, thirty, single, and pregnant again.

"Any questions?" Dr. Matthews asked.

How about, how had it happened this time? She'd been so careful, was so zealous about protection.

But obviously not careful enough.

She shook her head, just wanting to get this over with. Wanting to get the information she needed and get out of here. "No."

"Well, you're entering the honeymoon phase now. Second trimester is generally the easiest part of pregnancy. Your energy should be back, and sex shouldn't be a problem, either. In fact, lots of women say sex is better now than before they were pregnant." The doctor gestured. "Let your partner know that he won't hurt you, or the baby. Sometimes men get worried about that."

Noah would be one of the men who worried about something like that. Noah was a good man. He'd marry her if he knew she was pregnant with his baby.

He couldn't know.

But then, she hadn't told Bear, either.

"Are you taking your prenatals?" the doctor asked, rolling

back on his stool to reach for his iPad. The medical group had given up paper in favor of e-files. Apparently, everyone had gone electronic.

Savannah wasn't sure how she felt about it. But then, she wasn't sure of anything anymore, was she?

She sat up and pulled her top down, covering her stomach. "Yes," she said, answering the doctor. "Taking the vitamins. They make me queasy."

"They can. And the iron in them might constipate you."

"And they do."

The doctor smiled at her. "I'm glad you've decided to keep the baby. I know it was a difficult decision, what with your career. But babies travel. Your little one will get used to life on the road."

Savannah's smile never wavered. There was no way she could ask Dr. Matthews about options now. The laws had changed. She'd have to go somewhere far from here to have the procedure done. "And who is going to want to see a pregnant country singer on stage?"

"I'm certain you'll figure out how to dress to hide it as long as possible."

She slid off the table, smoothed her skirt down over her slim hips. They should be slim. She'd perfected starving herself. All the new country-western stars were thin. She wasn't a star yet, but she was thin, too. It was just a matter of time now before she hit it big. Her agent even said she was getting some traction. Her new record was getting played more than the first one had. With a little luck and continued hard work, she was aiming to hit the charts this time.

So no, there was no room for a baby in her life. She was just thirty. She had plenty of time for babies later ... should she even feel inclined to be maternal.

But to end another pregnancy?

She winced, uneasy. Her parents would die if they knew. Her dad was a pastor, and her mom was holier than him. Which was why she'd told no one about her pregnancy two years ago and wasn't about to tell anyone about this one, either.

But Noah would want the baby...

Savannah suppressed the little voice, not wanting to think about Noah, aware that he deserved better. Aware that he deserved someone like him ... someone loyal, loving, honest, kind.

Bear hadn't been kind. Bear had been tough. Bear had been fierce. Beautiful. Sexual. He'd been so unbelievably good in bed. She'd loved it. Loved the way he didn't take her attitude. Loved the way he tied her up, made her hot, made her come. She'd loved dancing with him. Loved walking with him. Running to him, from him, loved everything about him...

Until Tulsa.

Her eyes stung, and she blinked hard and leaned forward to pick up her purse. Couldn't cry, wouldn't cry. Stupid to cry over things she couldn't change.

Bear was the past. Noah was the present, and Noah was a good man. He tried hard to make her happy. That had to count for something.

Dr. Matthew's stool squeaked as he stood up, iPad under his arm. "We'll see you next month then. The front desk will get you on the schedule." He was heading to the door, reaching for the knob.

Tell him, tell him, tell him...

You don't want the baby. You need an abortion. Tell him...

Savannah cleared her throat. The doctor glanced at her. She hesitated, wishing she didn't care what people thought of her. Wishing she didn't care what she thought of herself.

Dr. Matthews waited, giving her a moment.

She had dreams, big dreams. There were things she wanted, places she wanted to go...

"Everything okay?" the doctor prompted, his hand still on the knob.

She nodded, slowly. "Yes."

But she sounded nervous, uncertain.

The doctor frowned and, pushing up his glasses, he turned away from the door to focus on her. "You're sure?" he said.

Tell him.

Tell him.

"Dr. Matthews," she started, then stopped, her throat dry, her mouth like cotton. "I ... I ... haven't told him." She reached up to push long honey hair from her face, tucking it back behind an ear. "The dad. He doesn't know." She frowned, struggling to find the words. "I don't … know."

The doctor's forehead creased. "You don't know how to tell him?"

She struggled to swallow. Her mouth was so dry. She licked her lips. Hated herself, hated what a coward she was.

"Yes," she said, grasping at straws, unable to say what she wanted to say. That she couldn't do this, couldn't have this baby, and yet at the same time, she couldn't bear to think about the life she'd be snuffing out.

THE DOCTOR'S EXPRESSION gentled. "Creating life is a beautiful thing. I am sure your boyfriend will be thrilled. He might need a minute, but with time, he'll be just as happy as you are."

She nodded, glad she hadn't told him the truth, glad she didn't have to witness the disappointment in his eyes. He was a doctor of life, not death.

"You'll be fourteen weeks next week," he said.

She nodded.

"You're not showing much yet, but you will be soon. My suggestion is to talk to your partner today. Go out to dinner. Make it a celebration. If he's the kind of man I think he is, he'll be pleased."

Leaving the medical office, Savannah walked slowly to

her car, sliding on her sunglasses to shade her eyes from the intense Tennessee sun.

She'd vowed she'd never do this again, go through this again. And yet here she was. Pregnant. Again.

There was no room for a baby in her life. Not now, not when she was beginning to have doors open and opportunities present themselves.

But to end another pregnancy?

Her parents would die if they knew. Fortunately, they'd never know. They weren't close, and she hadn't talked to them about anything real or important in years. Probably not since Bear's accident.

She hadn't told Bear about their baby, either. At least, not initially.

Savannah reached her car and slid behind the steering wheel, remembering how she'd told Bear what she'd done, how the truth had come out in a fight, a terrible fight, and that had been the end of her and Bear.

It was what she'd wanted at the time, her pain seemingly as great as his, only later … later she realized she'd made the two worst mistakes of her life—ending the pregnancy and telling Bear. If she hadn't told Bear, they might have worked things out. They might still be together today, because that was what she'd wanted. She'd loved him fiercely, passionately, and in a fit of passion, she'd screamed what she'd done, wanting him to feel her pain.

She'd been successful, because he had.

Now she was facing another impossible decision. Noah could at least provide for the baby—should she choose to keep it.

Noah would take care of them both. That was the kind of man he was. Loyal, honest, kind. If only he was her type.

She wasn't attracted to kind men. Bear had been gorgeous and tough, but she wouldn't have called him kind. Bear, being Bear, was ambitious and fearless, but not patient, and not doting. He'd been loyal, though. He'd also always been honest. He'd never cheated on her, and yet he'd never made her his world, or his focus. No, that had always been his career. He'd loved bull riding more than he'd loved her.

Savannah turned on her favorite country satellite channel, the Garth Brooks channel, and tried to quiet her thoughts. Her head ached and she felt heartsick. She didn't want to think anymore. She just wanted to forget.

Once home, back at the apartment she shared with Noah, Savannah opened her fridge, studied her beverage options, wanting a glass of wine, thinking it sounded really good, but she went for one of her peach ice teas instead.

Collapsing on her couch in the tiny but elegant living room, she sipped her tea and stared up at the ceiling fan, doing her best to avoid thinking of anything, not wanting to remember the doctor's pleased expression as he listened to the baby's heartbeat. Not wanting to remember how shitty she felt walking out of his office.

Men should be the ones to have the babies. Men should

have to turn themselves inside and out for reproduction. As it stood, they had things too easy. *Get hard, ejaculate. There you go. Done.*

She squirmed against the cushions, trying to get more comfortable. Her bra hurt. Her boobs were way too tender. She hated having Noah touch them, but she couldn't tell him why she didn't want him to touch them. And he was a boob man. Loved to pinch and knead and suck.

The pressure was back in her chest, the one that made it hard to breathe.

She didn't want to be the bad guy again. The bitch. The ruthless, relentless ball-breakin' female who only cared about herself... even though the description resembled her to a *T*.

Tears burned, itching her eyes, scratching at her throat, begging to get free. If only she didn't have such big dreams. If only she could be like other women, happy with hearth and home, a man, and kids.

If only she didn't need to sing and make everyone sit up and listen. God, she loved it when they got quiet and listened with their hearts and not their ears. She could feel it when the audience got it. She could feel it when they got her.

She was a good singer, too. She had a good voice. God-given talent. She booked gigs and had fans and traveled nine months out of the year doing her version of the circuit—opening for the big names at the big state fairs and playing the smaller clubs and honky-tonk bars in between.

The door opened, closed, footsteps sounded in the hall,

boots against slate tile.

Noah was home.

"Baby, you home?" he called from the entry.

She half-closed her eyes, listening to him set his keys down on the hall table, picturing him setting his hat next to the keys. Cowboys didn't hang their hats, they stored them flat. She hadn't known that when she'd first met Bear.

"In the living room," she called.

His footsteps quickened. He entered the room, tall, broad shouldered, his thick dark blond hair cropped close, emphasizing the strong angular lines of his face.

Leaning over her, he smoothed her hair back from her face and kissed her forehead, and then her mouth. "How did things go at the doctor?"

"Good." She smiled up at him, her smile artificially bright, hiding the tumult within.

She'd told him the doctor appointment was about her throat, her voice, and she'd told herself she did it to protect him, because Noah wasn't duplicitous. He didn't lie. He didn't pretend to be anything he wasn't. Not like her.

"No real damage to those vocal cords?" he asked, kissing her forehead again.

"Just a little strain, no polyp."

"What are you supposed to do for it?"

"Avoid smoking, drinking caffeine. The usual."

"But then it should be okay? No long-term damage."

She wouldn't even go there. She forced a smile. "Nope."

"That's great news." He smiled at her and then dropped a kiss on her lips this time, blue eyes crinkling. "I think we should go out somewhere tonight. Someplace special. Celebrate."

Celebrate.

She lifted a hand to his face, touched his cheek, his skin warm, a hint of beard rasping her fingertips. He had a nice face. It matched his pure heart. "We don't need to go out."

"But, baby, this is a big deal. You were so worried. Now you can still go on tour in a couple weeks."

Hurt just to hear Noah call the six-week, play-for-no-pay trip through the southwest her *tour*. She'd never imagined that after seven years in this business she'd still be struggling, sleeping on a retired school bus with the musicians while they drove all night to get to the next gig.

"I'm not so sure I want to go," she said, sitting up, rubbing the top of her head.

She wasn't nauseous anymore, but she still got headaches. She'd be glad when they stopped. None of the pain relievers touched them, but then, she didn't take the strong stuff. Just in case they hurt the … you know.

Noah sat down next to her, then pulled her onto his lap. "Why don't you want to go? You love performing. You were born to sing."

She was so close to him she could see the bits of green in his blue eyes. When Noah was emotional his eyes turned aquamarine. They weren't turquoise now, but they were beautiful. He was beautiful. And patient. Supportive. Interested in her, and her life, and her dreams. He was everything a girl wanted. Hell, he was everything her parents wanted for her. The man had faith. He prayed.

If only she'd met him before Bear. Things would have been different.

Yeah. She'd be married by now, with three or four little kids running around, tugging on her, crying for juice or animal crackers or whatever it was kids cried for.

But that wasn't the life she wanted. Staying home, taking care of kids, while Noah traveled on his circuit, riding bulls…

She didn't want to be home. She wanted the stage, the lights, the microphone. She wanted everyone to know her, to love her music. To love her.

Her daddy used to caution her against desiring fame, saying that fame was Satan's province. That no matter what one accomplished, it might not ever be enough.

Her daddy might be right about that.

She'd spent all these years in Nashville, and she could draw a nice little crowd on the right night to the right bar, but she wasn't a star.

She wanted to be a star.

And she would be. It was just a matter of getting out there, working hard, and being in the right place at the right time.

She leaned forward, kissed Noah. "Okay, let's go out.

You decide where. I'll go shower and change."

In the shower, Savannah turned her back to the warm hard spray and used her favorite scented gel, sliding the foaming cleanser over her breasts and belly, down her legs, under her arms as the hot water pulsed against her back.

In the morning, she'd call the clinic Dr. Matthews's nurse gave her and schedule the appointment. She'd schedule it for next week, toward the end of the week, when Noah would be gone. He'd never know. It'd be fine. Better for both of them.

The bathroom door opened. Noah entered, whistling. The sink faucet turned on. She could see him through the shower's thick bubbled glass standing at the sink, lathering his face with shaving cream. He always shaved before he went out at night even though he'd shaved that morning. Noah was Mr. Clean. *Make that squeaky clean.*

She laughed to herself, turned away, facing the showerhead to wash off the body gel.

She'd never liked guys like Noah. They were just too nice, too predictable, and predictable was boring.

Bad boys intrigued her. Bad boys kept her guessing. Bad boys were hard on her heart, but for some reason that appealed. It made love feel active. Like she was having to do something, which made her feel something, which made her feel. It was hard to feel sometimes.

She was never supposed to be with Noah this long. He was supposed to be a rebound. Just like the guy before him, and the guy before that. Noah was merely a way to get over Bear.

But she hadn't got over him, had she?

She still dreamed about Bear at night, and woke hoping to find him in her bed.

He wasn't. He'd left Nashville and her.

Not true. She'd left him, and then he'd left Nashville. And her. But it had been her decision to break it off. Her decision to want something else, someone else, someone not ... broken.

Just like it'd been her decision to terminate the pregnancy two years ago when Bear had been in the hospital, in a coma after his accident.

Savannah turned off the shower, opened the shower door, and reached for a towel.

Noah was there, putting one into her hand. "Thanks, babe," she said, mopping her face and her arms and legs before wrapping it around her.

As she left the shower, a naked Noah stepped in, taking her place. Her gaze swept him, assessing.

He saw and lifted an eyebrow.

She made a face at him as she went to the sink and mirror, pulling the elastic band out of her hair and letting the long, artfully highlighted strands fall past her shoulders, down her back.

She loved her hair, spent a fortune on it, and never regretted it. She'd always had long, golden hair. It was her trademark.

Like half of Nashville. But whatever.

Applying moisturizer, Savannah saw Noah in the mirror's reflection, too. He wasn't as tall as Bear, but he had a great body—big broad back, thickly muscled, tapering to narrow hips and his small firm ass. He wasn't hung like Bear, but at least he wasn't a pencil dick like the guy before him. Ugh. Jared or Jeremy or whatever his name was. He'd been a huge mistake.

Noah wasn't a mistake. But was he forever?

Bear was going to be forever, until he got hurt. Why did he have to get hurt?

She'd gotten the abortion when he was in his coma. The doctors weren't thinking he'd survive, and if he did, he'd never be the same. She couldn't handle such devastating news; couldn't cope with everything they were saying. It was better to end the pregnancy now, early, and she convinced herself that ending the pregnancy was the best thing for both of them. But later, when Bear was rehabbing, and the doctors told him it was unlikely that he'd ever be able to father a child, she felt guilty. Sick.

What had she done to him?

The months following the accident were hard. All those surgeries and therapy sessions—physical and occupational—the appointments filled the day. She stopped working so she could take care of him and play chauffeur, driving him from one appointment to another. She hated it. Hated how the accident changed Bear, too.

As time passed, he retreated from the world, retreating from her, disappearing inside himself and until they only had silence. Anger. Bear said he just needed time, but Savannah, having already spent six months on the roller coaster aftermath, wanted off the ride. She wanted out. She wanted normal. She wanted the Bear before he was hurt, not this new Bear that couldn't even reach the bathroom sometimes without losing control.

Leaving him at the end of nine months seemed efficient and practical. It was the clearest way to an end—literally.

She couldn't have a new beginning without the end, so she left, but she left still conflicted, still more than a little in love with him. One day, she'd get him out of her system. He was just a man after all. To help move forward, she'd find a new man. What was the expression, *the fastest way to get over a man is to get under a new one?*

She wanted sex, real sex, again. Wanted to get laid. Not cuddling, or romantic love making. But an old fashioned, hard, hot session on all fours. Or up against a wall. Or bent over the tailgate of a truck.

She wanted sex like she and Bear used to have.

So, she'd spend six months dating and being pursued—Noah being the most determined—and she'd played him and the others until Noah told her to make a choice. If she couldn't commit to him, he was done. He loved her but didn't enjoy being strung along. She liked this forceful

Noah. He reminded her of the old Bear. So, she dropped the others and moved in with Noah, but she still hadn't gotten Bear out of her system.

Maybe she never would.

Chapter Six

JOSIE WAS AT the design firm, pricing out windows for Neil when her phone rang. It was Rye, and he rarely called during the workday, so she took the call, hoping it wasn't about Jasper. He'd been doing well lately—so well that he'd expressed interest in taking classes at Gallatin College and working toward an economics degree.

"Hi," she said to Rye. "Everything okay at home?"

"Everything's fine. I normally wouldn't bother you at work, but I saw a house this morning that I thought might be good for Bear, but you know about accessibility better than me—"

"That's not true."

"Well, you know how to make a handicap accessible home look good, and this one doesn't."

"Ah."

"The house is in Marietta, one street off Bramble. To put it bluntly, the house is a little depressing, but the last person to live there was in a wheelchair and there is a ramp, a big kitchen, and a bathroom that would work for him. Doors are wide enough, light switches were lowered, doors feature handles not knobs."

"How do you know so much about it?"

"The realtor asked me for a quote on how much a new roof would cost, and he decided to go with my bid. We start work Monday."

"Is the house going on the market then?"

"The owner can't afford for the house to just sit there, so she's open to a yearlong lease, or a purchase offer."

The long lease would appeal to Bear. "Is anyone living there now?"

"No. It's been vacant for months, and there's been no offer."

"Priced too high?"

"Not for the neighborhood, but for the condition. It's the ugly house on the street, and it wouldn't take a lot for the seller to spruce up the front, but she's only going to pay for the roof and that's it."

"Is the roof that bad?"

"It's why there's been so much water damage."

"Has that been addressed?"

"No, but we will be next week. Should be sunny and dry for the next month. We'll get the roof off and replace all the rotted wood, beams, and so on."

"That bad?"

"Let's just say someone decided it was cheaper, and easier, to put buckets under leaks than to fix the problem."

"Does the interior smell funky?"

"Fortunately, no. But the interior is going to need fresh

paint, and some decent furniture—and fixtures—would help."

Josie glanced at the clock on her laptop. "I'd like to swing by and see the house. Do I need to call the realtor?"

"Nope. I have a key."

"I need to finish these numbers for Neil, but I could probably be there after lunch. Would one or one thirty work for you?"

"I'm just working down the street so call when you're close and I'll drive over and meet you." Rye rattled off the address and then said goodbye.

Josie set her phone down and leaned back in her chair, looking across the office, taking in the window, the framed awards on the wall, and the conference desk and chairs on the opposite side for team meetings.

Marietta wouldn't be a bad place for Bear. In fact, it'd be a really good place for him. He'd be close to downtown, right in the thick of things. The house didn't sound very appealing at the moment, but if the bones were there, and basic accessibility, she could do some quick touchups and inexpensively improve the aesthetics.

Maybe this was what he needed. Not just a place to be during the remodel of his house, but society. Company. Activity.

TWO HOURS LATER, Josie stood outside an uninspiring beige house, with the same faded beige trim. The house had probably been built between the 1940s and 1950s. A home without bells and whistles and fancy detail. She suspected this house had replaced an older turn of the century home, or maybe someone had subdivided their lot and built this to fill the lot.

Rye had been right about the lack of curb appeal, but curb appeal was one of the easiest things to fix, in her opinion. Plants would help. Maybe some window boxes. Nothing was green in the front, and the long sloping ramp needed paint as much as the windows. But the driveway's asphalt had been recently repaved, and the sidewalk to the front door only had a minor crack.

Rye pulled up in his truck as she was still taking inventory.

He parked in front of the house next to the curb and stepped out. "She's not much to look at," he said. "But it's solid, and except for the roof, and replacing the damaged drywall and wood in the back bedroom where the leak was, the house has possibilities."

"Kitchen and bath, too?"

"Let's just let you walk through." He unlocked the front door, pushed it open, and Josie followed him inside.

It was a warm day, but the interior was dark and cool. As her brother shut the door behind them, he switched on the lights, revealing a decent-sized living room with heavily curtained windows.

"You see the doorways are wide, and the hallway itself is wide, so there's no problem for Bear's wheelchair," Rye said as they walked from the living room to the dining room.

The dining area was a slightly smaller space in the living area but with ample room for a decent size table and chairs—and room for Bear, too. No one in a wheelchair wanted to be bumping against things, and Bear would want plenty of room to be able to turn corners and navigate the furniture. "A round table in here would be perfect," she said. "Bear could just roll right under it, and it'd still feel spacious in here."

"Check out the table in the kitchen," Rye said, leading the way into the kitchen.

The kitchen doorway had been widened in the past ten or fifteen years, the swinging door removed. There were scuff marks on the door frame but nothing that couldn't be covered by a little paint.

Like the house, the kitchen was designed for practicality, the old counters covered in laminate, and the cupboards looked like the original, painted a very pale baby blue. The stainless sink was divided in half. The faucets had watermarks but worked fine. The stove had seen better days, but the burners turned on. The white refrigerator worked, too, the interior cold.

Josie spied the old-fashioned booth in the corner, beneath the corner windows. The bench was u-shaped, and the table a rounded rectangle, with plenty of space at the end for Bear's wheelchair.

"He can prep here," Josie said, turning to face her brother.

"Or eat here, have his coffee here, whatever," Rye agreed.

"The only change I'd suggest is opening the space under the sink. Obviously, if Bear wanted to spend the money he could get new appliances, but everything seems to work."

"Just needs some freshening up. Paint and such."

"What about the bedroom and bathroom?"

"Not pretty, but utilitarian and it functions. Bear would probably want to change up the showerhead. Its old and there are a lot of good ones available that don't cost a fortune."

"Is it a roll-in shower then?"

"Someone tried to create a roll-in shower, but the tiles are lifting and there's some water damage. I suspect it wasn't sealed right. It might require some work but shouldn't be too bad. If Bear is interested in the house, I'd ask Richard, my plumber, to come in and have a look."

"It's as you said, functional but not attractive."

"Well, that's what you do, right? Style on a shoestring?"

"Since he's renting, yes. If he were to buy it, I'd suggest bigger changes."

Rye nodded. "He might want to buy down the road."

"I'll reach out to Bear and see if he can meet me here."

Josie not one to procrastinate, phoned Bear even before

Rye had returned to his truck. Bear didn't answer though, and disappointed, she left him a voicemail message. She was trying to decide if she should head back to Bozeman or wait a bit when he returned her call.

"Hi," Bear said. "I was on another call."

"No problem." She cleared her throat. "I'm in Marietta. I just saw a rental house that might work for you. Well, Rye saw it first and then asked me to come over as he wanted my opinion."

"You think I'd like it?"

"Well … there's potential.

"That doesn't sound encouraging."

"It's not a lot to look at now, but with a couple of changes, it could work well for you, and based on what I'm seeing, I'm sure the rent is affordable."

"Where in Marietta?"

"Almost downtown Marietta, just a few blocks off of Main Street. My brother was hired to reroof it, and once he saw the house, he thought of you wanting a smaller, more accessible place. I've got the key. Want to come see it?"

"Now?"

"If you're free. Otherwise, we can make it work for another time this week—"

"No, today is good. I can be there in less than an hour."

"I'll text you the address."

She sent the address and then messaged her brother. "Bear is on his way, I'll let you know what he thinks."

BEAR HAD BEEN poker-faced throughout the brief house tour. He obviously didn't love it, but he also didn't come out and say he hated it, either. He just maintained that blank, impossible to read expression.

"Well?" she said as they returned to the living room. "Thoughts?"

"How far is Bozeman from here?"

"Thirty to forty, depending on where you're going—and snow and traffic. But if conditions are good, thirty."

He nodded thoughtfully. "And why would I want to live in Marietta?"

"Because there are people nearby. And fun things to do here." She paused. "Have you looked at any commercial spaces here?"

"Not yet, but I did see something that looked interesting. The building is owned by Cormac Sheenan, brother to my friend, Dillion."

She lifted a brow. "That could be promising. When are you going to see it?"

"Soon, I hope."

"Why not today?"

"I don't have an appointment."

"That might not be an issue. Call and see if someone can show you around. Why not? Tell them you're here now."

Bear's lips twitched as he fought a smile. "Do you ever

rest?"

Josie thought a moment and then, grinning, she shook her head. "No."

He laughed and pulled out his phone. "At least you're honest."

THE FARRELL BUILDING was one of the older properties in downtown Marietta, just off Main Street, behind the sheriff's department. The building, one hundred years old, featured red brick and sturdy stone masonry, along with a decorative cornice with the number 1910, proclaiming its age. The large two-story building had served many functions over the past century, with retail and sales on the first floor, and apartments and offices for Montana's growing business class on the second floor.

Unfortunately, a fire gutted most of the second floor in the Farrell Building ten years ago, and Cormac Sheenan had cleared out the debris when he bought it but hadn't done much else. He was there to walk Beae and Josie around the ground floor as the realtor wasn't available, but he seemed eager to see the Farrell Building be put to good use again.

"I bought the Farrell eight years ago," he said. "It was my intention to use this as an extension for my media business, but there were some delays, and then Covid, and by the time the world had returned to a normal, I discovered that my company didn't need all the office space we'd initially thought was so essential."

"Your employees liked working from home?" Josie guessed.

"Loved it," he answered with a laugh. "But then, I did, too."

"And so the building has just sat here for years?" Bear asked as they returned to the entrance, which had probably once been stately glass doors but were now boarded over like the other narrow windows on the side facing the street. The opposite side of the interior had no windows as it was snugly attached to another larger, turn-of-the-century building.

Cormac nodded. "I own the whole block, but the office building next door is currently leased for another five years."

"Good, because I only need the one building," Bear said, "and this is pretty perfect, but it's going to come down to the terms."

"I understand." Cormac hesitated. "Put an offer in, and let's see what we can do. I'd like this to work. I support what you want to do."

Bear shook his hand and then, as Cormac opened the door, wheeled out with Josie at his side.

She'd been unusually quiet during the half hour spent exploring the Farrell Building and Bear was curious to get her thoughts now. "Have time for a coffee?" he asked.

She nodded. "An iced one," she said. "It was hot in there."

"It was warm," he agreed. "I have a feeling there's no air conditioning."

They walked the three blocks to Java Café, and it was relatively empty as it was four o'clock now and nearing the end of the business day.

"What did you think?" he asked as they settled at a table with their beverages.

"It's a big building."

"I know, but I liked that. I could see dividing the space into private offices at the back, with the front being the facility for the clients."

"You'd have to offer plenty of accessible bathrooms and those would eat up space."

"How many do you think are necessary?"

"It depends on how many clients would be training at the same time, but you might want two large private bathrooms, plus an additional private bathroom with a shower. Just in case."

Not following, he lifted a brow and then understood what she was saying. "That's probably smart. Accidents happen."

"Someone might also need to go straight to another appointment, and I imagine it would be easier to shower here than go home, clean up, and head out again."

"Maybe two regular bathrooms, and two bathrooms with showers," he said.

"Or one regular accessible bathroom, and two accessible

with showers."

"Would you be interested in being the designer?"

"For my design projects for school?"

"For projects for school and as a job. I'd pay you—"

"I'm not supposed to take paid outside work. Its part of my contract with the design firm. I can do jobs that meet the requirements of my school projects."

"We don't have to tell anyone."

"Yes, we would, including the government. I pay my taxes, Mr. Anderson."

He lifted his hands in surrender. "I do, too. But I'd love to have you work with me on this, and my house—"

"You don't have either, yet."

"I will soon," he said confidently. "It's just a matter of getting the numbers to line up, and they will. Now, will my house and the SCI facility work for your projects? What is the criteria?"

"It can be residential or commercial, or both. The objective is to create a universal space in each, with strong, commercially appealing design elements." She smiled, expression hopeful. "I would love to work on both your projects. I love that they're different from the other. It's pretty exciting."

"It is," he agreed.

"But you don't have an agreement for either one, so I don't want to get excited only to be disappointed."

"The house isn't an issue. It's very plain which makes it

very affordable," Bear said dryly. "I'll have Rye send me the owner's info tonight and get that one squared away."

Josie frowned. "But if it's a rental property, do you really want to put money into it? The owner is the one who'd benefit—not you."

"I'd benefit. I'd be living in a considerably more stylish home."

"And have nothing to show for it after a year." She hesitated. "I don't know your financial situation, but if you were able to get someone to lease the ranch property, could you afford to buy the house? Perhaps finance the Farrell Building and get a mortgage for the house? Or, depending on your situation, buy the house for cash and it might be easier to get a better mortgage for the commercial space.

"How did you become so knowledgable? And practical?"

"I've loved houses since I was a little girl, and then I spent far too much time eavesdropping on Mom and Dad's depressing conversations about money, and the lack of it." She smiled grimly. "But I learned a lot, and I'm a big believer in smart, stylish, *affordable* design."

"Which fits my budget. So, are you in? Want the job?"

"Yes." She showed him her fingers, which were crossed. "Provided my advisor says yes, and I can't imagine she wouldn't."

"Keep me posted," he said.

"You, too. I'll be dying to know how all of this plays out."

IN THE END, it was Rye who called and told Josie that Cormac had accepted Bear's offer for the Farrell Building after a minimal back and forth, and that Bear was also the proud owner of a 1948 house a block from the grand Bramble House.

"You mean, he's leased the house?" she asked, confused by Rye's wording.

"No, Bear bought it, and because he was paying cash, he got a great deal. As well as the new roof the previous owner had just paid for."

"That is pretty sweet," she agreed, still trying to process her brother's news though. "So just to be clear … Bear got both properties?"

"Yes. In the same week."

For a moment, she couldn't think of anything to say. When Bear took action, he took action.

"Are you still there?" Rye asked.

"I'm just stunned. A couple weeks ago, Bear didn't know where he was going to open his first location, or where he'd be living, and now he's invested in the Marietta community."

"I think it's a good place for him," Rye said.

"I do, too. Now, I just need to get that final approval and I can get to work on both projects. You do know that Bear asked me to oversee the design for both."

"I'm not surprised. He obviously respects you."

Josie blushed, her face hot. She was glad her brother couldn't see. "The feeling's mutual," she said lightly.

"You know, if you're going to be working a lot in Marietta, and it sounds like you will, you're always welcome to stay over with Ansley and me. We'd love to see more of you."

"I'd love to. It'd be fun to get to know Marietta better."

"I have a feeling you'll soon know the town a lot better."

After hanging up, Josie flopped back on her little loveseat in the little sitting area of her studio. So, Bear was now the proud owner of a house and a very desirable commercial building—well, eventually it'd be desirable. Neither place was exactly a dream at the moment, but she could see his vision and she was excited to work with him on both.

As well as excited to spend more time with him.

She loved being around him, and even though she'd tried so hard to analyze her feelings, she couldn't. Why was she so invested? There was no reason for her to care this much.

She didn't know if it was the fact that he was a legend in Montana or that he'd been a world-class athlete before he'd been hurt.

She didn't know if it was because he was incredibly attractive, truly one of the most beautiful men she'd ever seen in real life, or because he'd once had so much and now, he was confronted by permanent limitations, never mind other people's narrow opinions.

She suspected it was a little of everything, because she did find his situation tragic. The knowledge that he'd been so badly hurt, and was fighting so hard to reclaim his life, touched her, moved her.

Her mother would say it's because Josie had such a tender heart, but it was more than that.

Her feelings weren't platonic. She was attracted to Bear and had begun to spend an inordinate amount of time thinking about kissing him and being kissed by him. He'd be a good kisser. She was sure of that. She lightly touched her fingertips to her lips, her upper one so sensitive that her belly clenched.

Bear had said he couldn't have children, but did that mean he couldn't have sex? Did it mean he wouldn't enjoy making out or foreplay?

On one hand, it wasn't any of her business, but on the other, she was curious. And hopeful. Hopeful that one day he might feel a little of what she felt for him.

Some people might not be comfortable with Bear's paralysis, but it didn't seem strange to her. Her brother had been born with a birth defect that changed his life. Her father, a tough, tough man, broke his back by falling off a roof. Both people were wonderful people. Both had physical challenges, but it didn't change who they were.

Bear just felt like her person. Like hers.

Josie wished she could talk to someone about it, and thought briefly of her sister Hannah, but Hannah could be rather ruthless. She was practical to the extreme. Having had enough of poverty growing up, she was dating an older man—an unattractive older man—because he had money.

Hannah denied it. She said she loved him. But the rest of the family found it hard to believe. Hannah was stunning—could easily pass for a model—and so why would she be with an older, plump, balding man when she could probably have anyone?

No, Hannah wasn't the one to talk to. Josie and Hannah were nothing alike. Hannah was pure ambition and Josie far too tenderhearted with an overwhelming need for justice.

Josie's mom used to lecture her about being so sensitive. She shouldn't be drawn to the heartbreaking stories, or feel compelled to do something for everyone, but Josie did. She always had. Even as a little girl, she'd wanted to help those in their community who needed more—more support, more kindness, more respect.

Growing up, she was always doing one fundraiser or another, collecting bottles and cans, volunteering, writing letters and making calls—even showing up at city hall to talk to whoever was in charge.

Josie had never felt self-conscious about any of it. Nor had it ever crossed her mind that she shouldn't, not even when one of the city councilmen she'd had approached—a car dealer with a car lot not far from Calhoun Roofing—and said she was following up on the donation she'd written him a letter about. When Mr. Clark said he didn't get a letter, she pulled another one from her notebook and handed it to him to read.

She watched him as he read her carefully printed letter, and then came to the end and looked up at her. "You're a Calhoun."

She nodded.

He chuckled, there really was no other word for it, and shook his head. "Shouldn't you be doing this for your own family? Seems like your dad needs more help than anyone else in this town."

Josie stood there, twelve-turning-thirteen and full of anger and disappointment. If he'd hoped to embarrass her, he'd failed. She felt embarrassed for him—and terribly disappointed. Disappointed that someone who was in a position of power, a person who could easily do something, would instead choose to make fun of her dad. It wasn't hard to help. It wasn't hard to give. He could have just donated a dollar. Five dollars. It wasn't even the amount of money. It was his attitude. His air of superiority. And so, she stared him down, smiling just a little bit, smiling because he with his money and car dealership and position on the city council was not even half as good of a human being as her dad.

"You could have just said no," she said, smiling a little bigger. "You could have said it wasn't a good time for you to give. You didn't have to make fun of him, especially as he's the first to give when someone needs help. He always has been. And I'd rather be like him then ever be like you."

She walked out of his little office in the small city hall and marched down the steps, back stiff, head high, even as her heart raced and her legs quivered. She was still unlocking her bike when a woman came rushing out of the brick building, her pink heels clattering on the sidewalk.

"You're doing a good thing," she said breathlessly, thrusting a twenty-dollar bill at Josie. "And don't you let anyone tell you otherwise.

"And you're right about your dad. He's a good man. He always was the first to help everyone. You're right to be proud of him. Don't ever let anyone make you feel small." She patted her chest and then her middle. "People like to make other people feel bad about themselves. But God loves us no matter our size, no matter our talents. Just remember that when someone is hurtful. Keep doing God's work."

"Not really trying to do God's work," Josie said. Her family wasn't particularly big on church, not anymore. They'd gone fairly regularly when she been younger but that had all ended after her dad's accident. "I'm just doing what everyone should do. Care about your neighbor."

"That's right. That's exactly right. Love thy neighbor." The woman turned and returned to the building, hustling again. Heels clacking, her pink and purple dress the only bright color on a dreary spring day.

Josie rode her bike to the roofing office not sure if Rye would be there or out on a jobsite. But he was there, working away on his laptop and making notes on a pad of paper. He smiled at her as she approached his desk. "Already done with your homework?" he asked.

She shook her head, exasperated. "It's spring break, Rye. There's no school this week."

"Heading to the library then?"

"No. I've been trying to get donations."

"For who this time?"

"The animal shelter. They just took in a bunch of cats and kittens. They have to spay and neuter and microchip and stuff like that so the kittens could be adopted."

He set down his pen. "Josie, you don't have to do everything."

"Not doing everything. I'm just trying to help a little bit."

"You know, Jo-Jo, you can't save everyone."

She shrugged. "But I can try."

Swallowing hard, Josie pushed away the memory and rolled off the little couch in her studio apartment. The memory had made her sad. Maybe sad wasn't the right word. Maybe she just felt ... conflicted. She knew she was a little bit different from others, but it was a good thing. Not everyone was supposed to be the same.

Chapter Seven

IT WAS A good week for Bear. Cormac apparently was as eager to sell the building as Bear was to buy it, with Cormac accepting Bear's first offer, agreeing with alacrity to the proposed thirty-day closing. Now that Bear had his desired commercial space, and his house, he was free to move into his new home in Marietta anytime, and the big brick building would be his at the end of the month giving him time to get plans drawn and permits filed. Finally, he was moving forward, and his plan to have a facility for SCI people wasn't just a dream but soon to be a reality.

A huge weight felt as if it had been lifted off Bear's shoulders and for the first time in months, he slept well, and woke up refreshed.

The days passed quickly, filled with appointments and meetings, not just with Rye and his subcontractors, but with city officials and a local venture capitalist—introduced to Bear by Cormac Sheenan—who was intrigued by Bear's idea.

He was hoping to get Josie involved soon. She was finishing up her midterms for her two summer school courses and then promised to turn her attention to Bear's projects, as she'd just gotten approval from her advisor who seemed as thrilled by the two design opportunities as Josie was. It probably helped that she was doing the design work for Bear Braden Anderson, everyone's favorite local legend.

She told him that on Friday when she drove to Marietta to meet him at the house. He had the keys now and was hoping to move in sooner than later, but Josie wanted him to wait until they got the big stuff done.

"You don't want to live in the middle of a remodel," she reminded him, "even if it's a small one. Wait to move in until we at least get your bathroom done, because they're going to tear out the floor and plumbing and retile it. It's going to look nice when they're done—it'll be a proper wet room with tiles on most of the walls. I know Rye will do his best to manage his subs, but the tile saw is noisy, and small spaces can be particularly chaotic. You didn't want people in your way in Clyde Park, and it'll be even worse here. Everyone will be on top of each other."

"True," Bear agreed. "I'm just ready to be out of the ranch house."

Josie nodded sympathetically. Now that she knew Savannah was such a part of the house, she understood his motivation for getting out sooner than later. "We're tackling the bathroom first. With luck you can be in within ten days. Maybe two weeks."

RETURNING TO HER apartment that evening, Josie discovered an envelope had been slipped under her door. Inside, she picked up the envelope and drew out the typed letter.

Her apartment lease, as well as the larger apartment next door, would not be renewed at the end of August. The owner had plans for the building and after three years of applying for permits and jumping through the planning commissioner's hoops, the owner had gotten permission to turn the two upstairs apartments, and the attic above, into a rooftop bar.

Josie supposed this was good news for Bozeman's business district, too, but it wasn't good for her, or her neighbor. Her neighbor was a pilot with Montana Air and rarely around, but Josie was around, and she'd liked her spot in downtown Bozeman. It had been nice to walk to everything, from class to shops to her favorite coffee spot two blocks over.

She could always move home, but that didn't appeal. She'd loved her independence, and being on her own had made her realize how sensitive she was to the family drama. Her dad was doing better than he had in Eureka, but he still had his moods and down days.

She could possibly live with her brother but that didn't have much appeal, either. She loved Rye, but he was so protective—overly protective—and she didn't want to have to be explaining to him where she was going every time she left the house. It was one thing to stay over now and again, and another to make Rye and Ansley's home hers.

Josie pulled out her laptop and began checking for available apartments in Bozeman. Most one-bedroom apartments ranged from $1,900-3,000 depending on how new and luxurious the complex was. But she didn't need a complex with a pool and gym and community center. It wasn't as if she'd be showing up for Saturday barbecues or Hump Day Happy Hour on Wednesday.

After some searching, she did find an apartment in an older complex for $1,200 a month. It wasn't big, but it had everything she needed, meaning a kitchen, bedroom, bathroom, and a tiny living-dining space just big enough for a card table and her loveseat.

Josie put in a call to the phone number on the listing to see if the unit was still available, but her call went to voice mail. She left a message asking if unit 4A was still available.

She was still scrolling through Bozeman housing listings when her phone rang, and she reached for it hoping it was the apartment manager but wasn't disappointed when she saw it was Bear.

They talked a lot, and they were both so open with each other, that when Bear asked her what she was doing, she didn't think twice about blurting out her situation, and how she was bummed to lose her current spot but already searching for a new one.

"You can have one of the bedrooms at my new place," he said. "If you're going to be working so hard on my projects—"

"Theoretically they are also my projects."

"Precisely. You might as well live where you work. Although I can also see why you'd prefer Bozeman. It's closer to your family and friends."

"I'd be closer to Rye in Marietta," she said thoughtfully, "and it'd be fun to see more of Ansley. But wouldn't it be … awkward?"

"How so?"

Josie hesitated, and frowned, not sure how to explain. "I've never lived with anyone except my family."

"No roommates during college?"

"No. I've been in a studio apartment this past year, and when I wanted to, I headed to my parents' house."

"Do what's best for you. I just thought you might like to be living closer to your two job sites."

"What about you? Won't you hate having me around so much? I'm sure I'll end up getting on your nerves."

"I'd rather you be here than some stranger. I'm picky about housemates. I like things clean. I know you. You're not a lot of work, and I'd never have to give you the no drinking, no smoking, no parties lecture."

She laughed. "Oh, you don't know me. I could very well throw parties every weekend. Live bands, dance floor, keggers, you name it."

"I'd like to see that."

"No, you wouldn't." She thought about his offer, not

sure if he was truly open to renting her a room. "But are you serious? About renting me a room?"

"It's a three-bedroom house. I don't need three bedrooms, and I'm not going to rent you a room. I'm going to give you a room. If you're working for free, you should at least have free room. Don't you think?"

"I do like saving money."

"Take your time to decide, because there are negatives for you. You'd be driving to Bozeman for work, and then you'd have to deal with me, and I'm not always Mr. Cheerful."

"I'm nearly done with the internship and my classes wrap up the end of summer, which means I just have my projects." She paused, smiled. "And I'll buy you a flag, maybe a pirate flag or a bear flag and when you're in a bearish mood, you just hang the flag and I'll know to steer clear."

"You're hilarious," he said dryly.

"I know. I make myself laugh."

"When do I see you again?" he asked.

"Tomorrow afternoon. I'm coming back to measure for your new appliances."

"I'm doing new appliances?"

"The new washer and dryer, remember?"

"Oh, yes, I do, and if you think you can squeeze a dishwasher into that kitchen, measure for one of those. I hate doing dishes by hand every night."

"I'll work on it."

JOSIE MADE PLANS to meet Ansley for a quick early lunch as Ansley's gallery didn't open until noon on Saturdays as she stayed open until ten in the evening.

They met at Rosita's, the Mexican restaurant on Main, and both ordered the chicken taco salad with extra guacamole and wasted no time diving into a proper catch up as it had been over a month since they'd seen each other. Ansley shared that she was busy painting, working at the gallery, and spending an evening or two each week with her uncle on his ranch. Her brother Lachlan was still there, and he'd settled in well, and was thinking that the Campbell ranch in Paradise Valley should break even at the end of this year, and with luck, be profitable the following year.

"That's not luck," Josie said as their salads arrived. "That's hard work."

"He's happy there, and that's the good thing."

"It's also great that your uncle Clyde gets to stay in his house. He has to love that."

"I can't see him in a senior home," Ansley agreed. "He'd be so difficult."

"How is his health?"

"Up and down. Some days are good, and some days he's just so childish. He's beginning to have tantrums and thank goodness Lachlan has a cool head. He doesn't let Uncle Clyde get to him. But he will need more care as time goes on. Probably full-time care."

"Which is expensive."

"The money isn't the issue. It's getting my uncle to agree to anything." Ansley shook her head. "Enough of that. I find it rather depressing. Let's talk about you. You must be so excited to finally have your design projects squared away. You've got six months to work your magic. Can you do it?"

"If I had to rely on any other contractor than Rye, no. But Rye is so good, and we work well together. It makes me happy to team with him." Josie pushed some of the lettuce around, uncovering bits of corn and cheese. "I have a question for you."

"Oh?"

"If I lived in Marietta, could you put me to work?" Josie asked. "With it being summer, you have significantly longer hours and I'd be happy to come in and do some evenings or work on the weekend. I know you have someone who helps you out part-time, but you wouldn't need to pay me—"

"Of course I'd need to pay you! You're already working for free for Bear Anderson."

"That's different. It's part of the requirements for my design project, but I'd feel weird taking money from you."

"What if we worked it out so that you'd earn a percentage of everything you personally sell? That way it's a win-win." Ansley gave her a penetrating glance. "My work isn't inexpensive. They don't just walk out the door."

"I think it sounds fun, and it would give me something

to do on the weekends, and evenings."

"But isn't that a lot of driving back and forth to Bozeman? Or are you thinking you'd like to stay with Rye and me this summer? You'd be more than welcome. We have plenty of room and Rye has already said to your parents that he doesn't want you driving late at night. He worries about drunk drivers and people not being responsible."

Of course Rye did. Rye had become everyone's surrogate father after their dad was injured and gave up on life.

It crossed Josie's mind that now was the time to tell Ansley everything. Josie would need an ally and she hoped Ansley would be that person. "Bear has offered me a room in his house, and since I'm going to be spending so much time in Marietta, I've accepted. I won't be paying rent, so I'll also be saving money."

Ansley didn't immediately speak. Her gaze dropped and she seemed to be concentrating on her salad, but Josie knew Ansley was stalling for time. Seconds continued to pass, a tick ticking that Josie felt in every bone in her body.

"You don't approve?" Josie asked, forcing the issue.

Ansley's shoulders shifted. "It's not for me to approve or disapprove. You're a grown up. You can do what you want."

"Yes, but you're usually so enthusiastic about everything and I'm not sensing any enthusiasm from you." Josie watched her sister-in-law's face closely. "What are your concerns?"

"Wouldn't you be more comfortable with us?" She

looked at Josie now, her expression uncertain. "I mean, I'd love to have you stay. Rye would, too."

"I have thought about it, but you're both outside of town, and I am excited about being in town. Bear's new house is an easy walk from Main Street, as is the Farrell Building, and I'm looking forward to walking everywhere and exploring Marietta. It will also be helpful when I need to meet one of Rye's subs or be there for a delivery."

"Does your brother know your plans?" Ansley asked.

"Not yet, but I don't think he'd mind. He likes Bear, and the fact that I'm no longer costing anyone rent should be a plus."

"You've always chipped in and done your share," Ansley protested. "This last year in particular. You were working full-time while also going to school full-time. I don't know how you did it."

"It helps that I love design, and I get excited about every project. But it would be fun to do something a little different this summer, and being here in Marietta would be like a summer vacation. I could help out at your gallery. I could make some friends—"

"Maybe go on some dates," Ansley added. "You haven't had a social life since I met you."

It was on the tip of Josie's tongue to confess that she had feelings for Bear, but at the last moment managed to hold back the words, realizing Ansley wouldn't welcome the news, and no one in her family would probably be that thrilled, either.

She forced a smile, hiding her turbulent emotions. "I like the idea of working for you on commission. I think it's ideal."

"But I can go days without selling anything. Some weeks paintings move quickly, and other weeks, they just hang there."

"I don't mind. It's a challenge and you know I love those."

"Oh, I do."

"And just think if I can sell one of your huge canvases"—Josie lifted a hand—"that would be amazing. Just know, I'm not wanting a big percentage. Whatever you think is fair is good with me."

Ansley gave her a long look. "Can we talk about Bear for a minute?"

Josie's smile slipped. "Sure."

"Why are you moving in with him and not us?"

Josie didn't know how to answer. Eventually she just shrugged. "I think it'd be fun."

"Fun?"

"We're friends. We have a good time together."

Ansley didn't appear convinced. She kept studying Josie, as if waiting for her to crack. "Rye thought—and he could be wrong—he is a man after all. But Rye thought you might have a crush on Bear."

Josie had two options. Be honest or keep pretending that

Rye and Ansley had it awrong. "I might," she carefully admitted. "It's hard not to be a little smitten. He's smart. Gorgeous. Successful."

"And how does he feel about you?"

She sighed. "Brotherly?"

"You're sure?"

Josie nodded. "He said I remind him of his sister Susie."

"So, he keeps an eye on you. He'll keep you safe."

"Absolutely." Josie could tell Ansley was relieved. Josie wasn't sure how she felt. "But if I'm being perfectly honest, my *crush* is one of the reasons I thought it'd be good to get out in the evenings and weekends. It's why I'd love to work in your gallery. I don't want to just be hanging around the house every evening and weekend. It's a small house, and one day it'll be a charming house, but I do need a social life, and if I'm working in your gallery, I'm going to be meeting people and having something to do." *Besides crush on Bear.*

"Are you sure that moving in with Bear is the right next step for you? It's kind of a big step."

"That sounds really weird when you put it that way. I'm renting a room from him—more or less. There's no torrid affair."

"He's still a mature single man, and your family is pretty conservative."

"No more conservative than your family, and definitely no more protective than your brothers. Poor Rye having to face down the five Campbell brothers at one time."

Ansley grinned, obviously enjoying the memory. "I was very impressed at how well he handled them. But then, Rye never shows fear."

"Probably because he's not afraid of anything—except something happening to you."

Ansley's expression softened, turning tender. "I am madly in love with that man. He wasn't as convinced that we would work. Fortunately, I had you and Hannah on my side."

"Always." Josie reached across the table and gave Ansley's hand a quick squeeze. "Now I have a talented sister that's going to put me to work. Right?"

"When do you want to start?"

"A week from today? Next Saturday?"

"I open at noon."

BEAR'S LITTLE HOUSE in Marietta was coming along nicely. His bathroom was nearly done. The new appliances were installed in the kitchen and the tiny, enclosed porch at the back of the house had become the new laundry room. She'd insisted the washer and dryer slide into their new spot without a frame or box beneath, and then had a slab of marble installed over the appliances, giving Bear a solid work surface for sorting laundry or folding clothes. Josie was also careful to document every step and decision for her program.

Her bedroom was ready for her to move in. Rye knew she would soon be moving, but her parents didn't yet know. She hadn't yet broken the news to them, and she wasn't looking forward to it. But with her moving out of her studio in just days, it was time to share her plans, and she had to do it face-to-face.

Josie made arrangements to have dinner with them on Thursday night, offering to bring their favorite Italian dishes—cheese ravioli with meat sauce, lasagna, baked rigatoni—plus garlic bread and a bottle of red wine.

Her mother had set the table and Jasper, slumped sideways in his electric chair, used his laptop to show Josie the courses he would be taking at Gallatin College in the fall. "I might need an aide," he said, struggling to form sentences.

Josie knew not to hurry him because eventually he'd get the words out, and even if they weren't clear to strangers, she understood them.

"The school said they could help me maybe," he added.

"I'm excited for you. You've wanted to go to college for a long time."

"I've taken classes online but it's not the same."

"No, it's not," she agreed. "It's probably lonely doing it online."

"And boring." He leaned forward a little, his mouth opening and closing, his facial muscles straining with the effort to speak. "I need to get out. Parents making me crazy."

Josie laughed and kissed him on his forehead. "I totally

understand."

They headed to the dining room for dinner, and it was a pleasant meal, with everyone in a reasonably good mood. Her dad seemed healthier—and happier—than Josie had seen him in a while, and her mother shared that her dad had been getting some physical therapy himself and was discovering that he was stronger than he thought and had even begun to think about some woodworking activities he could do again.

"Rye said he could build your dad a new work bench," Mom added, "but Dad says he wants to do it himself. He just needs Rye to pick up the lumber and maybe lend a hand here and there."

Josie's eyes widened. "Dad, this is fantastic. Remember the jewelry boxes you made for Hannah and me? I still love mine. Maybe you could make one for Ansley for her birthday."

Her dad nodded. "That's a good suggestion. It'd be a good first project for me."

"Don't start with something too difficult," Mom cautioned. "You don't want to get frustrated and give up."

Dad's smile faded. "I won't give up."

Mom seemed about to protest but Josie jumped in first. "I have some news," she said brightly.

Everyone looked at her, and Josie drew a breath and gathered her courage. "I'm moving to Marietta. I'll start moving things in tomorrow, and Rye has promised to help me get everything else on Saturday."

"You're going to live with Rye?" Mom said, head tilting.

"No, Rye's just helping me move. I'm going to be renting a room from Bear Anderson. Since I'm working on his two projects in Marietta, it seemed most practical to stay in Marietta, and he had space, so it's all arranged."

Her mother reached for her wine glass and took a sip. "You have a place, Josie. You have a nice place of your own. Why move in with him?"

"I've lost my lease. I'll soon be forced to move out, and Bear is giving me a great deal. I won't have to pay rent, so I'll be saving money."

"I'd feel more comfortable if you'd live with Rye and Ansley. Have you discussed this with them?"

"Yes, and they offered to let me stay, but I don't want to move in with them. I'm excited to have some independence. I also think it'd be fun to have a roommate. Except for my sister, I've never had that before."

"Say housemate," her dad interjected gruffly. "Because you won't be sharing a room, I presume."

"That's true. I'll have my own room and my own bathroom. Well, my bathroom is the one guests would use when they come visit but I don't know who would come visit at this point other than Rye and Ansley."

Her mother's brows pulled. "But, Josie, you barely know the man."

"I've been working with him for the past month, and so

has Rye. Rye likes him, and thinks Bear is a trustworthy person. Call Rye. Talk to him. Ask him. You know Rye's always been a good judge of character."

"I'd just be more comfortable if you were living with Rye. He and Ansley must be past the honeymoon stage now. I'm sure they'd welcome you with open arms."

Do not roll your eyes. Do not. No matter what you do…

"Mom, this is about me wanting to do something new, and I think it'd be a fun adventure living in Marietta for the summer—"

"Just the summer?"

"Probably the fall and winter, too, if all goes well. I'm looking forward to walking downtown. They have farmer's markets every week until the end of September, and apparently Marietta at Christmas is just magical. The whole town decorates, and they have so many festive activities. We never did any of that in Eureka. I've been working hard, too. I'll be graduating soon and I'm going to be working even harder once I'm out of school. Best of all, I'm going to pitch in at Ansley's gallery, and if I sell her works, I'll earn commission."

Josie's parents exchanged glances.

"But you wouldn't be doing this if it weren't for him," her mother persisted. "You would still be in Bozeman focusing on you and your dreams, instead of thinking about his."

"I am focusing on my dreams. I can't graduate without my design projects, and my advisor was tough to please, but she approved the Farrell Building project and Bear's house, and if it weren't for his invitation to join his team, I wouldn't be graduating in December."

Her mother just kept shaking her head. "I think this is about Bear. I think you're taken with him and caught up in his tragic story."

"It's not that tragic, Mom. And yes, I'm designing for him so that he can function independently in his own home, but this is what I love to do. It's what I want to do for everyone—whether or not they have a disability."

"Not disabled," Jasper said, grinning. "Able."

Josie blinked back tears as she smiled at Jasper. Thank goodness for his sense of humor. Otherwise, she'd be a mess right now. It frustrated her to no end that her mother didn't listen to her, and that everyone in the family seemed so determined to wrap her up in gauze and keep her from harm. But that wasn't life, and life had risks, and she refused to hide away just so she wouldn't get bruised or broken.

"I don't think it's a bad thing to care about others," Josie said after a moment. "I don't think it's bad to choose to be supportive."

"Josie, I understand you have a big heart, but I can't approve of this, and I don't support it."

Josie bit into her lip, holding her breath, reminding herself she'd expected pushback. Her mom was a worrier and worried. Her dad had struggled with depression for years. They'd lived on a painfully tight budget, a budget which meant that Josie and Hannah hadn't been able to go to college right away after high school. They'd both spent a year or more working and saving up every penny to put toward their tuition and books.

Until a year ago, she'd lived with her family in Eureka. She'd only moved to Bozeman for school and the internship, and even then, Rye had checked out the apartment to make sure it was safe for her.

"So, you're going to be his roommate, is that it?" Her father asked, his dark brow furrowing, his gaze meeting hers.

"As you pointed out, I'm not sharing his room," Josie said evenly. "I'm essentially renting a room in his house. There will be nothing weird, nothing for you to worry about. Bear will just be my landlord."

"I don't like it." Her mother's voice sharpened. "And you can say what you want about there being nothing weird, but I'm not comfortable at all. Your work is in Bozeman. Your classes are in Bozeman—"

"I'm done with classes in just a few weeks. My internship is wrapping up as well. I hope Melissa and Neil will offer me a paid position with them, but they haven't said anything yet, and might not want to."

"Why wouldn't they?" Jasper protested. "You're brilliant."

"Because they can just get another intern and work her or him to the bone, and not have to pay." Josie wrinkled her nose. "That doesn't sound very nice, and I like Melissa and

Neil a lot. I'd love to stay on there. I just don't know that it will happen."

"Josie, honey, you're my born optimist, and I love that about you, but nothing about your plan makes sense. It's just not logical. Staying with your brother would be the logical choice."

Josie shrugged helplessly. "Sometimes what we want isn't logical—"

"Your dad didn't expect to fall from the roof. We never thought he'd break his back. Who knows what could happen to you if you are driving to Bozeman every day? Who knows what might happen when the weather changes? There are so many accidents every year, things out of one's control. I can't have anything happen to you. I just can't." Mom glanced at her dad, eyes bright with tears. "Tell her, John. She's always listened to you."

Josie looked into her dad's eyes, looking as she always did—deeply, with love—because when others gave up on him she never did. "Nothing is going to happen to me, Dad," she said quietly, gently. "It's Bear who is hurt. I'm fine. I'm good. You don't have to worry about me."

"We love you, Jo-Jo."

"I know, Daddy, and I love you and Mom. I love Jasper. I love our whole family. But I have to do what my heart is telling me, and my heart is telling me this is the right move." She reached over to take her mom's hand, but her mother pulled her hand back. "I won't be driving to Bozeman every day, and if Melissa did offer me a position, I imagine I could work remotely a couple days a week. I work remotely some days now."

"I think what your mother isn't saying," her father said at length, filling the long silence, "is that we don't want you to end up being a caregiver. It's not been easy for your mom, and we had plenty of good years before my accident."

"Bear isn't helpless."

"He'll have serious health concerns as he ages—if not now. If you don't believe me, talk to Hannah. Do some research."

"That may be, but he's not sitting around feeling sorry for himself. He's trying to improve the lives of others with spinal cord injuries. I respect what he's trying to do. And he's good company. He's fun."

"I'm sure he's fun right now," her mother said, folding her napkin and placing it beside her dinner plate. "But just wait until he's in the hospital with a serious infection. It won't be fun then."

Chapter Eight

BEAR DIDN'T SUBSCRIBE to print newspapers, and only scanned the news outlets' online headlines once a day and rarely turned on the evening news. So, he'd missed the breaking information about the enormous pileup on the highway in western Idaho yesterday afternoon caused by heavy smoke from a wildfire in southeastern Oregon.

It was jarring reading about the disaster this morning, a day after it had taken place. It seemed that the smoke, combined with morning fog, created whiteout conditions resulting in a tractor trailer and a tanker colliding. The tanker overturned, burst into flames, and vehicles crashed into one another, with several trapped underneath larger ones. The spokesman from the Idaho Highway Patrol shared there were quite a few fatalities, but they had no final headcount due to the difficulty extracting cars and people from the carnage.

The story was so grim, it was the headline on virtually every American news outlet, and after reading several versions of the story, some with conflicting details, he forced himself to turn to the sports page to focus on something less tragic.

But the freeway pileup remained on his mind, as well as everyone's mind. Throughout the day, different people mentioned it to him. Rye said something while they were standing outside Bear's house waiting for the electrician, and then the electrician mentioned it the moment he arrived. The tile layer said it was awful beyond words. At lunch, Flo at the diner mentioned it. Everyone was worried as the death toll rose and rose and rose.

Bear had just returned to his Clyde Park ranch when Jimmy Jenkins, one of his longtime friends from the rodeo circuit texted him, sharing that Noah Kamp had never shown up for the rodeo in Pendleton yesterday. Noah was driving the 84 through Idaho yesterday, at least that had been the route he'd told his friends he was taking, and Jimmy hoped Bear had maybe heard from him.

Bear hadn't. Confused, Bear reread the text. What was Jimmy saying? That Noah was missing, or that Noah was maybe involved in the pileup?

His hands trembled slightly, something they'd never done before his accident, making texting challenging. Giving up on typing the words, Bear called Jimmy. "When was Noah supposed to arrive in Pendleton?"

"Yesterday." Jimmy sounded tired and hoarse. "He'd planned to arrive by three at the latest."

"When was the last time anyone heard from him?"

"Yesterday morning. Noah called Pete from the road and said he was making good time and should be in Oregon around eleven thirty, and at the fairgrounds by three."

"He was definitely driving the 84 then."

"Yes."

A sickening heaviness filled Bear's gut. "And no one has heard from him since then?" Bear persisted.

"Not that I know of."

Bear held his breath, wanting to imagine other alternatives. Perhaps Noah's truck had overheated, or he'd needed to be towed for a repair. Maybe Noah had lost his phone. Maybe he'd caught a stomach bug and had pulled over at one of the highway rest stops...

But even if one of those was true, Noah would still communicate. Noah was the most reliable, responsible person Bear had ever known. "It doesn't sound good," Bear said at length.

"No, it doesn't," Jimmy agreed.

"Keep me in the loop."

"I will."

In his bedroom, Bear stripped and wheeled into the bathroom, the doorway wider. The painters had applied a primary coat to the new door and frame and had touched up the baseboards and filled the hole, but still needed to return to give a final coat, but they were waiting for Bear to move out to do it.

After a shower, he dressed and took his iPad into the kitchen where he filled a glass with water and pulled up the Highway 84 tragedy on his device, reading every article he could. He poured over the facts, and since it'd been over a day since the accident, the details were clearer. It was estimated that between forty-five and fifty vehicles had been involved, including seven big rigs, but investigators were working on the exact numbers, which was proving challenging do to the fiery explosion from the tanker and semitrucks. The freeway was still closed in both directions and probably wouldn't reopen for another forty-eight hours, if not longer.

Bear called Noah. No answer. He texted him and waited, pacing restlessly in the kitchen, rolling back and forth, turning sharply, to roll the opposite direction.

Noah would answer. Noah had to answer. He'd talked to Noah just a few weeks ago and everything was going well for him. He was having his best year on the circuit in years, winning big money, gaining new sponsors, and he and Savannah were going strong, too. Noah rarely mentioned Savannah, and Bear didn't ask, but Bear had been glad for Noah, glad that Noah, who had once been one of his best friends, was doing well. Noah deserved to be happy.

Bear rolled backwards until he bumped into the refrigerator and sat motionless, thoughts tangled, pulse racing. He felt sick, nauseous, exhausted. There were just too many accidents, too many tragedies, too many deaths.

Noah had to be okay. And just like that, Bear thought of Mick, Noah's dog, an Australian Shepherd mix that usually went everywhere Noah would go. Had he been in the truck at the time? And what about the horses?

Part of Bear didn't want to know more, but another part of him had to know.

The person who might have the answers was Savannah. She was also the last person Bear thought he'd ever call, but in light of the tragedy, he couldn't not reach out.

Savannah answered after the third ring. "Bear," she said, her voice pitched low, husky with emotion. "You've heard the news."

"What have you heard?"

"The sherriff's office called an hour ago. They've identified Noah's truck and trailer, and Noah, too." Her voice cracked and she pushed herself to continue. "He had his wallet on him. He made it easy for them. His dad is going to fly to Boise to recover his remains."

Bear held his breath, trying to wrap his head around the news. After an endless silence he forced himself to speak. "How are you?"

She laughed, the sound strangled. "Terrible."

"I am so sorry, Savannah."

"Me, too. And now I have a dog—"

"You have Mick?"

"I do, but I can't keep him. I can't take care of a dog. I can't even take care of myself."

"I'll take him."

"You will?"

"Yes."

"You mean that?"

"Yes."

She exhaled. "What about the baby, Bear? Do you want that, too?"

He didn't answer. He couldn't think of an answer. She was joking, right?

"I've shocked you," she said, voice rising, cracking again. "But it's true. I'm pregnant, Bear, and now Noah is gone, and he'll never know he was going to be a dad."

"You hadn't told him?"

"No."

"Why not?"

"I wasn't sure I was going to keep the baby."

"Oh, Savannah."

"I know. *I know.*"

"Don't you think it's time you stepped up and did the right thing?"

"Don't judge me!"

"I'm thinking of Noah. I'm thinking of what he would have wanted. This isn't a handbag, it's not something—"

"I can't raise a baby on my own," she interrupted fiercely.

Bear had heard all of this before. He'd known when they were dating that hearth and home didn't have the same appeal as performing and glitzy costumes, but he hadn't imagined she'd be so quick to get rid of their baby. "There are plenty of good people who'd love to be parents."

"You're talking about adoption."

"It's the right option if you don't want to be a parent yourself."

She said nothing.

"How far along are you?" he asked.

"I don't want to talk about it."

"Maybe you should. Maybe it'd help you figure out a way forward, a way where you can honor Noah's memory without giving up your dreams."

"I can't be pregnant. I'm booked all summer. I'm traveling all summer."

"There's no reason you can't do both. It's not like you're riding a bronc."

Savannah fell silent again.

Bear suppressed his frustration. How could he have thought she was the one for him? How had he not known who she really was? "When is your due date?"

For a moment he didn't think she was going to answer.

"Early January. I'm fifteen weeks." Then she was crying, crying hard.

Bear said nothing, because what could he possibly say?

After a minute, the sobs eased and her breathing steadied enough for her to whisper, "They say karma's a bitch, and now I know what they mean."

THE REST OF the afternoon was a struggle, and it didn't get

easier for Bear. He thought of little besides Noah, and what a good friend Noah had been to him following Bear's accident. Noah had come to visit him daily in the beginning, and then weekly between Noah's travel schedule.

When Bear hadn't wanted to continue the painful rehab, Noah had got into his face and told him to man up and do what needed to be done, reminding Bear that he had a fiancé and a future, and it wasn't fair to Savannah to just give up.

Bear's sister Susie had also come from Australia and said much of the same thing. But there was something powerful in Noah's reminder that real men didn't quit, which stayed with Bear, focusing him.

Noah might have gotten Bear back to his physical and occupational therapy, but it was Susie who provided TLC since Savannah had her music and couldn't make it to the hospital daily.

Susie, staying in one of those Residence Inns with little kitchens, would make Bear's favorite chocolate chip cookies, or a berry crisp, substituting their Montana huckleberries for blackberries and boysenberries.

Susie had hand after hand of cards with him, and while they played, she told him her favorite stories of when they were growing up, and not the grizzly story, but what it was like growing up as kids living in a national park, thanks to their dad's job as a US Park Ranger. They'd spent most of their years in Yellowstone and the Grand Tetons, but there had also been a stint in the Badlands, and Glacier National

Park.

They reminisced about their different schools, and how their mom had tried to homeschool them one year, but Bear had ordered copies of the teacher's edition and used it for his homework and reviewing before tests. He got the best grades of his life that year and the only one who knew what he was doing was Susie, and she never told.

Susie and Noah were the ones who got him through that first year. Savannah put in appearances, but she didn't know how to handle the accident, and his paralysis, particularly the mishaps that came with learning how to transfer, how and when to use the bathroom, how to even dress.

In one of their terrible fights when he demanded to know why she just kept disappearing on him, she cried and blurted that she didn't know how to cope anymore. It wasn't personal. She just needed a strong man.

THE NEXT FEW days were some of the worst in Bear's memory—at least since he'd woken up in the hospital from his coma to discover his world was forever altered. Everyone asked Bear if he'd known Noah Kamp. Strangers on the street offered him sympathy for the loss of his friend. Friends from his days on the rodeo and PBR circuits reached out to him, wanting to grieve with someone.

It was a lot. And he wasn't handling his own grief well.

Bear retreated to his ranch in Clyde Park and was grateful when his phone rang and it was Cormac Sheenan calling to ask if Bear had leased his ranch property yet as he knew of someone looking for a place like Bear's. It was a young family, and they'd be in town for just another few days, and they were hoping to test out living on a ranch before buying.

Bear hadn't yet had time to advertise his ranch and told Cormac to pass his contact info on to the couple, and that he'd be more than happy to have them come out and look around.

The couple followed up almost immediately and, grateful for the distraction, Bear invited them out for the next day. They settled on a morning time so that the family could still make their flights back to Los Angeles.

Aware that he hadn't been upstairs in years, he had no idea how the bedrooms and bathrooms looked. He called Josie to ask if she'd do him a huge favor and come over to the big house and walk through the rooms upstairs and downstairs, checking to see if everything looked and smelled fresh. He had a personal pet peeve about closed, stuffy rooms and didn't want the family to troop upstairs to be overwhelmed by claustrophobic heat.

Josie agreed and arrived with takeout from the Chinese restaurant in Marietta that was next door to the theater. While she dished the Kung Pao chicken, fried rice, and chow mein, Bear opened two beers and they ate on the front porch with the warm breeze blowing and the temperatures slowly dropping.

"This is sure pretty out here," Josie said, comfortable in a folding chair that she'd found in the garage, her gaze fixed on the rugged mountain range before them. "But these mountains aren't part of the Absaroka or Gallatin ranges, are they?"

Bear shook his head. "No, the Crazy Mountains are their own distinct range. They're nearly completely surrounded by private lands, which makes public access to the mountains difficult."

"I read somewhere that the Crazies, or Crazy Mountains, comes from a Crow name, but wasn't sure if that was true or not."

"I've heard two different stories, and both relate to the Crows. In the first, the Crazy Mountains is apparently a shorter name from the original, Crazy Woman Mountains, after a Crow woman who lost her mind, after losing her entire family in the westward expansion. Heartbroken, she disappeared into the mountains to live out the rest of her days alone."

"That's very sad. What is the other story?"

"The Crow people called these Ominous Mountains, with the English translation roughly being Crazy Mountains. Apparently, the mountains were known to have metaphysical powers and a place used for vision quests."

"I'm glad you're not in a hurry to sell your place. I worry that you might one day regret it."

"You know this house isn't my favorite."

"I do," she said. "But you have four hundred acres. You could build a new house for yourself anywhere."

"And what would I do with this place?" he asked, jerking his thumb to the big log cabin wall behind him.

"Make it a vacation rental," she said promptly. "I've looked at other local listings and you could earn some significant money renting it out, provided you required a four-night minimum or something like that. And then when you wanted to have a family gathering, you just block off those dates and reserve it for Susie and her husband and kids."

"Why do I feel like you're eager for me to invite Susie and her family here?"

"Oh, I am. I'd love to meet her, and I think she'd be so proud of you, founding a business that will benefit so many who couldn't afford this service without you."

"I've hinted at it, but she doesn't know yet. I am going to wait until the Marietta facility opens, and then I'll send her a link. Maybe a video."

Josie nodded, her brows tugging together. "Can I ask you something that isn't any of my business?" she asked after a few moments.

"When has that ever stopped you before?" he teased, reaching out to pluck a tendril of hair from her lashes.

Her cheeks turned pink, and her eyes glowed a luminous lavender. "I know, if I think it, I just say it."

"I like that. I find it refreshing."

"I am really impressed with what you're doing, Bear, but it struck me that you're not going to be able to make money from this venture. I don't see how you could if you're trying to make the service affordable—and available—for people who couldn't normally use one."

He didn't answer immediately, too busy just looking at her and drinking her in. She was everything he'd never thought he'd find in the world, and yet here she was—beautiful, compassionate, smart, funny, *kind*.

Bear couldn't think of one thing he didn't like about her. He loved her honesty. He valued her curiosity and directness, gratified that she thought about what he did, and took the time to understand his business model. Savannah had never cared much one way or another about his investments. Savannah had wanted him successful, wanted the financial security, but there were never questions about sustainability, or the ethics of something. For her, making money was black and white. The goal was to make money, not spend it.

"I decided years ago that I don't have to make money off of every business I'm involved in," he said. "Opening robotic centers for those with spinal cord injuries is something I have to do—whether or not it cuts into my revenue."

Josie nodded, eyes still shining, lips still curving. "I totally get it," she said softly, fiercely. "I think that's why I love what I do, create designs that even out the playing field for those who have challenges that not everyone understands, or cares to understand."

"Not everyone has empathy," he said.

"But it's more than that, don't you think? In my experience many people don't want to think about how much harder life is for those with a chronic illness, or a disability. I don't think people want to be uncaring, but many are just overwhelmed by their own problems. They don't have the capacity to take on the challenges others face."

She suddenly frowned and looked up at him, meeting his gaze. "There are times I can't bear to think about the life my mom leads, taking care of my younger brother and my dad. It doesn't seem fair that she has two people so dependent on her, but she doesn't complain. She just gets on with it."

"I have a feeling you're a lot like her."

Josie paused for a long moment. "I hope I'm happier. She's never complained about her life, but she's also never seemed … happy. And I don't mean joyous, bubbly happy, but she strikes me as sad. Or perhaps it's resigned. I never want to be that way. I never want to give up my power or feel like a victim. No matter what happens."

"I respect the sentiment, but it's a lot harder to keep that positive attitude when you've suffered significant losses."

"That's true." Josie crinkled her nose. "I'm not trying to judge her. Or anyone. I just know what it felt like growing up in my family, and how isolating it was. We didn't have very much money, and my parents couldn't afford help, so there were no days off for Mom, no self-care days, either.

Hannah and I tried to pitch in and help as much as possible, but there are some things kids just can't do for their parents."

"Like make them happy?" Bear said gently.

She nodded. "We can't make anyone happy," she said after a moment. "That's something we have to do for ourselves."

They were both silent for a stretch of time, and it was a very easy silence, comfortable, warm, peaceful. Sometimes Josie found it hard to relax, but there was something so restful about Bear. She felt good with him, herself with him. "Does everyone like you as much as I do?" she asked.

He laughed. "No. Definitely not. Most people think I'm a bear."

"Like your namesake."

"Mmmm."

"You can be grumpy," she said sweetly, "but I'm seeing less and less of that side of you. I think you're making progress."

He laughed again, and the sound gave her such pleasure. His laugh was deep and rumbly and impossibly sexy. "You're ruthless."

"I think you like it."

"Do I?"

She nodded. "You like that I don't take you too seriously. You like that I can make you laugh. And you like that I've put the right toilet in your new house so you won't fall off it again."

"I do think you're good for me."

She flashed an impish smile. "I do, too." And then she remembered something she'd been wanting to ask him, and it seemed like a good time now. "I've been dying to ask you, but is the story true, about how you earned your nickname Bear?"

He shook his head. "I can't escape that story, can I? It's been what … twenty-something years ago?"

"Everyone's heard it. In school, you learn about Lewis and Clark, Johnny Appleseed, Paul Bunyan, Daniel Boone and Bear Anderson."

He laughed, amused. "That is some strange history you were taught."

"I recognize some of those might have been legends," she said primly, "and some were real people, but you, Bear Anderson, are both a legend *and* a real person."

He gestured to his wheelchair. "As you can see, I am more man than legend."

She leaned toward him. "But did the bear *actually* attack you?"

Bear pushed up his sleeve showing his bicep and a glimpse of the deep claw marks scarring the skin of his shoulder. "It goes down my back."

"That's … wow."

"It got me pretty good. I wouldn't have survived if my sister hadn't run for my dad. Dad came charging with a rifle, and shot at the grizzly, and I lived to tell about it."

"But you jumped in front of your sister."

"I don't know if I jumped in front of her or pushed her behind me. But we were walking and suddenly there was the bear, and she was closer to the bear and Susie froze. Goofy lost his mind, barking and growling and dancing around the bear. I was afraid the grizzly would kill my dog, so I grabbed a branch and charged."

"Weren't you scared?"

"Terrified. But nobody messed with my dog. Goofy was my best friend."

Josie grinned. "So, you really were saving your dog and not your sister."

His eyes creased at the corners, humor warming the silver-gray irises. "See, you know the truth. It was never about my sister."

He was teasing her, but it wasn't his words that made her heart thud, it was his smile. His smile was so warm and intimate that Josie felt a flutter in her middle, a delicate tingly butterfly sensation. "I suppose it does make a better story if it was your sister."

"One hundred percent."

Josie couldn't stop smiling, even as the fizzy sensation inside of her rose, bubbling up in her chest. She felt a little silly, a little giddy, and very happy. "How old were you?"

"Ten. Susie was eight. And Goofy was five."

"What happened after your dad arrived?"

"He shot at the bear, but the bear took off."

"And then?"

"Mom called for help. Dad stayed with me while help arrived. I was airlifted to the hospital and got rushed into surgery where they fixed me up, and when I came to there were newspaper reporters, photographers, and congratulations from the governor of Montana." He gave her a look. "I was a really big deal. For all of one week."

"And the boy became a legend."

Chapter Nine

JOSIE LEFT CLYDE Park just before nine. Summer in Montana meant lovely long, light-filled days, and it was still light as she drove home, the roads relatively empty. But even then, she drove carefully, paying attention to the other drivers when they approached, but before long she was turning off Highway 89 for Marietta. A few blocks later she was parking in Bear's driveway and letting herself into Bear's house. The house smelled of paint, floor stain, and polish, and Josie cracked open the windows to let in some fresh air.

She'd spent much of the day painting the living room, and she examined the chocolate-colored walls, wondering what Bear would think. She liked them, and once the furniture arrived next week, she thought he'd like them, too.

This afternoon while the paint dried, she finished installing an accent wall in her little bedroom. Now that she knew Bear owned the house, she wasn't afraid of investing a little capital and elbow grease into turning the bland house into something more welcoming. The exterior was still rather hopeless, but that could come later, after Bear had moved in, and if the young family touring his house tomorrow wanted it, she knew he hoped to move to Marietta by the end of next week.

She didn't blame him. His Clyde Park house, so stunning and luxurious, hadn't been designed with a wheelchair in mind, forcing him to live in a corner of the enormous living room, and his bedroom—the former trophy room.

She still hadn't mustered up the courage to ask where all the trophies and awards had gone.

When she had asked him why he didn't go outside and enjoy his front porch more, reminding him that it would be a great place for dinner or his morning coffee, he'd answered in that dry tone of his that he hadn't yet mastered the art of rolling with plates on his knees, or a hot drink between his thighs when there was a threshold, and the front door had a significant threshold.

She, who understood the challenges of wheelchairs better than most, had forgotten this.

Josie suddenly pressed a fist to her chest, just above her heart, pressing back against the ache she felt. She felt oh, so many things, and it was scary caring this much. Scary wanting someone that had different needs than hers, that would never know the spontaneity so many took for granted.

Bear had to think for his body, had to create habits and patterns, learning to be aware for a body that couldn't signal pain or pressure, whether it was on his butt, his calves, or his bladder.

But he was also so much more than a man in a chair. He was larger than life and made her believe in the human spirit, and the resilience of man, and tonight, Bear had said all the things she believed—that there was more to life than just making money, and more to being alive than getting ahead. There was helping others, extending a hand to those who needed it. She believed in improving things for those she met. She wanted to positively impact the world around her. Maybe she was a hopeless idealist, but that was okay. It helped balance those who were hopelessly negative … and the world had plenty of those.

BEAR DID A last set of curls in the garage on his workout bench, focused on the muscle contraction and the burn. He was getting stronger, and he liked that he was gaining size. Perhaps, once he moved to Marietta, he'd join a gym. They'd had far more equipment than the bar, bench and dumbbells he kept here.

The move to Marietta was happening soon. It was just a few days now. He hadn't been to the house in days as Josie had forbidden him to visit until she had everything set up. She claimed she needed to take some photos for her project and needed to do that without his stuff cluttering it up, but he suspected it was more than that. He suspected she was doing her thing—decorating, fluffing duvets, and filling the living room couch with pillows no one needed.

The idea of her fluffing duvets and plumping pillows

made him smile. He was looking forward to living with her, seeing her daily, even if it was just in coming and going. Fortunately, they'd be working together on the Farrell Building, which would officially be his on Monday, and the permits had been fast tracked by city hall, allowing them to begin construction the first of August.

It was all coming together. Life was good. Better than he'd expected or hoped.

Bear finished his workout in the garage and returned to the house to shower and dress before heading to dinner in Marietta with Josie, Rye, and Ansley. Rye had booked reservations at the elegant steak house on Main Street to celebrate the Farrell Building closing on Monday. Bear had no intention of letting Rye pay for the dinner, but he definitely felt celebratory and was pleased that Rye recognized that this was a special occasion.

He'd just eased his jeans on and was starting to button up his western dress shirt when the doorbell rang. Was it the doorbell? He never had visitors and he couldn't imagine who was at his door at five o'clock on a Wednesday.

But there it was again, the doorbell, and it rang several times, an insistent peel that was impossible to ignore.

Bear rolled out of his room and down the hall to the front door. He was stunned when he opened it, looking up into a very familiar face, the face of someone he'd once loved. "Savannah, what are you doing here?"

She pushed a heavy wave of blonde hair back from her

face. Shadows circled beneath her brown eyes. "I brought you Mick." She turned to her dusty compact SUV and whistled. The dog pushed his head out of the half open driver's window. "See?"

"I told you I'd make arrangements to have him picked up."

"I waited for you to reach out, but you didn't—"

"It's only been a week."

"Almost two weeks," she corrected, "and you know me, I'm not good at waiting for things to happen."

So very true, he thought. "You should have texted, reminded me. There was no need to drive all the way here."

"I know, but I had to do something. I couldn't just sit in that apartment and wait for Noah to walk in the door. He's not coming back."

Her words were like a punch to his gut. He exhaled hard, struggling to catch his breath.

"No," Bear managed after a moment, the grief rising up, the injustice of it all as overwhelming on the day he learned his friend was gone. "He's not."

"And so, I'm here."

Bear ground his jaw tight, conflicted, angry, heartbroken. And yet, also relieved to see Noah's Mick looking healthy, the dog's black and white head hanging out of the car, his tongue lolling.

Savannah was another story. She didn't look well, too thin, and clearly sleep deprived. She wasn't his problem either, and the last thing he wanted was her here, on his doorstep—or anywhere else in his life.

She'd burned so many bridges, and Bear was bitterly sorry Noah was gone, but Bear wasn't in any position to help Savannah pick up the pieces. "You have family. You have parents. You have Noah's parents, and I know they'd be there for you, thrilled to help welcome his baby—"

"I'm not going to tell them," she interrupted tightly. "Not telling anyone."

"You told me."

"Because I already know what you think of me. It can't get much worse."

"So, what do you want me to do? Forgive you of all responsibility? Decide how you're to handle the future? You're almost thirty years old, Savannah. You're an adult."

"Thanks, Bear, super helpful."

Despite the shadows beneath her eyes, despite her alarmingly slender frame, she was still pretty, still Savannah, her long blonde hair tumbling over her shoulders. Her roots were darker than he remembered, but he also knew it was the style to do that. She was so meticulous about her hair color that it couldn't be by chance.

"I'm not trying to be an a-hole," he said. "But we haven't talked for years and now you're here, and I'm not sure why."

"That's not true. We talked a couple weeks ago. You called me."

"To find out about Noah."

"And I told you he was dead." Her voice cracked. Tears filed her eyes, the golden-brown irises framed by thick, black-mascaraed lashes. She averted her head, straight white teeth catching her lower lip. "And then I told you about the pregnancy."

"You said you didn't know if you wanted to keep the baby."

"Exactly. It should be my choice. I don't need my parents weighing in, or Noah's family weighing in, or *you*." She looked at him defiantly, the tears now clinging to her lashes. "But that doesn't change the fact that I'm scared, and I don't know what to do. Which is why I'm here."

"To not get my opinion," he said, and yet his anger was gone.

She was, and always had been, impossible.

Savannah blinked and wiped her eyes dry. "Can I just stay here? For a little bit? While I try to figure out … the future?"

"I'm getting ready to move. I'm out in just days."

"What? Why? Where are you going?"

"Marietta, it's about thirty-five minutes from here. I've bought a house there—"

"What's happening to our house?"

Our house. He held back a laugh. She would always be the main character in the story, and not just her story but everyone else's. "I don't know what I'm going to do with the house long-term, but for the next year I have somebody who's going to lease it. They're excited about living here, and that makes me feel good about leaving."

"But why do you want to leave?" She glanced past him down the hall toward the soaring great room with its majestic, beamed ceiling and stone fireplace that reached up all the way to those hand-carved beams. "This is the most beautiful place I've ever seen. And you poured your heart into it. You were obsessed with getting it right."

"For you, too, not just me. It was going to be our family home, but I'm single and this isn't exactly wheelchair friendly." He kept his tone light, not wanting to get into a lot of conversation about a decision he'd already made. "The folks who are leasing it from me have a couple kids and they've always wanted Montana property, and this will give them a chance to figure out if they'd like to live here fulltime or not."

"They sound like LA people. Actors or something."

"He's a director."

"I knew it." She shook her head. "It just seems wrong." Her hair swished as she looked up at him. "Do you need money?"

"Doesn't everyone need money?"

"I just didn't know if this move was motivated by financial issues."

"It's really none of your business, Savannah? You have your finances. I have mine."

And then he saw her stricken look and felt like a jerk.

She'd just lost her boyfriend. She was pregnant. She was ... just being Savannah.

"Rather than let the house sit empty, I thought it was better to create some revenue, as that revenue can go a long way in helping me with a new business I'm starting."

She nodded once and glanced away again, giving him her profile, which was stunning. She was a beautiful woman. But not his woman and hadn't been for a number of years now. He opened the door wider and rolled back a foot. "Did you bring any dog food for Mick?"

"Of course. And his bowls, and his bed, and toys." She drew an unsteady breath. "So, Noah's dog is welcome, but I'm not?"

"I don't think it's a good idea."

For a moment, she looked utterly lost, and whether it was real or manufactured it still got under his skin. She'd put him through hell, but she was going through it now, and he just couldn't kick her when she was down.

"It is getting late." he said gruffly. "So you can stay for the next day or so, but when I move out at the end of the week, you need to have a plan on where you're going next. You obviously can't stay here with the new family moving in, and the house I'm renting isn't big enough for the three of us."

Her head turned, thick golden hair swishing. "Three? Who else will you be living with?"

"Again, none of your business."

"Do you have a girlfriend, Bear?"

"I do not have a girlfriend, but my roommate is a girl."

"And the house has only two bedrooms?"

"The house has three bedrooms, but the smallest bedroom is going to be my office."

"You couldn't put a sleeper sofa in that room? Or one of those fold out chair beds? It'd give me a place to crash for a while."

"*No.*"

Her shoulders slumped, her entire frame crumbling. "Bear, I'm desperate. I'm not doing good. My thoughts are crazy. I feel crazy. *Please.*"

"It's not fair to Josie. It's a big enough move—"

"Can I talk to her? Before you decide for her, can I at least talk to her? Let me explain the situation? It wouldn't be forever. Just a little bit. Just until I get back on my feet."

"What about your music, and all your summer concerts? Noah told me about your schedule. He was worried you both were so busy you wouldn't see each other."

"My busy was lots of small county fairs, and small outdoor stadiums. Nothing significant. Nothing that will impress anyone in Nashville."

"It'll help pay some bills."

She nodded. "True." She hesitated. "But if I keep the baby, I can't do what I'd planned. Too much travel, too many late nights, too much stress."

"So, you're thinking about keeping it?"

"I'm thinking about where I could live until I deliver it. But no, not keeping it. There is no way I could keep it."

"The baby."

"It." Her eyes locked with his. "Don't torture me, Bear. Don't make this harder than it already is."

He lifted a hand. "Not trying to torture you, but Noah's family should at least know. His parents might want his child—"

"Stop. Please? I've driven for two days and two nights and I can hardly see straight. If you want to hammer me on ethics, let me at least get a good night's sleep."

"Fair enough We don't need to figure all of this out now. Get your bag, come in. We'll talk more later. Okay?"

She nodded, lashes wet. "Thank you."

He looked up into her face, feeling like a pushover, wishing he'd told her no, wishing he could tell her to get lost, but he couldn't. Not the way things were now. Not with Noah gone.

"I'm doing this for Noah," he said quietly. "And for his baby. Not because you and I have anything between us, as there's nothing here, nothing left. Not even a friendship—"

"I got it," she said, unsteadily, pushing a long, light tendril of hair from her face. "No need to hammer it in. You don't like me. You don't respect me. You don't trust me. I got it. But I'm thankful anyway. Now, I'll get my bags and get out of your way."

"And Mick. Let's let him out of the car, shall we?" It was

only then that Bear remembered his dinner plans with Rye and Ansley and Josie that night. The celebration dinner in Marietta.

He couldn't go now. There was no way he could go. The desire to celebrate was gone.

JOSIE GOT THE text at five thirty last night that Bear had to cancel dinner and asked everyone if they could please reschedule for next week once the purchase had closed.

Rye and Ansley agreed. Josie agreed, too, but she was disappointed. She'd been excited about going on a double date with her brother and sister-in-law, even though it wasn't really a date, but it still had felt special.

But now it was morning, and she was out for a walk, trying to get some exercise in before she ended up at Java Café for a coffee and one of their delicious homemade cinnamon rolls. The ring of her iPhone interrupted the music she was listening to, but she didn't mind when she saw it was Bear calling.

"Morning," she said, slightly breathless from her brisk pace.

She'd chosen a different route this morning, walking first to the end of Bramble where she entered Crawford Park, passing the library to the trail that followed the river. She walked the trail through the park, over the bridge to the fairgrounds and had just turned around to head back when Bear phoned.

"Morning," he answered. "Where are you?"

"Heading to Java Café. I tried a new walk this morning. It was along the river and very pretty."

"How far are you from Java Café?"

"Not far at all. Why?"

"I'll meet you there."

"Has something happened?"

"I'll see you in a few minutes."

Bear beat her to the coffee shop and had ordered her favorite latte along with her favorite cinnamon roll. She didn't even know he knew what her favorites were, but they were waiting for her when she arrived. "What brings you to Marietta so early?" she asked, joining him at the little round table in the bay window.

Bear propped his elbows on the edge of the table. "Savannah is at my house."

Josie couldn't follow. "Savannah."

"My former fiancé."

Josie's lips parted before she made an effort to press them closed. His ex was staying with him?

As if reading her mind, he added, "Just for a few days."

"Did you know she was coming?"

"No. She showed up yesterday late afternoon. She'd been driving for a couple of days and was beat. I didn't feel right sending her away and putting her back on the road."

Josie nodded slowly. "I get it."

"Do you?"

She nodded again. "My brother Rye would do the same thing. You guys are moral guys. You're the good ones."

"Not that good, Josie. Especially when it comes to Savannah." His brow creased, his jaw set. "I'm not happy she's at the house. I'm not comfortable with her around. We had a complicated relationship, equal parts good and bad, and in the end, it was just bad."

"But you were going to marry her."

He nodded once. "We had booked the reception, paid a nonrefundable deposit for the band, mailed the save the date cards. But then I was hurt, and it changed everything. We'd always had a fiery relationship, and when it ended, it truly imploded."

"If that's the case, why did she drive all the way here from Nashville? Or is there someone else in the area she's hoping to see?"

"She brought me a dog."

Josie went silent. Bear wasn't surprised. He was springing one thing after another on Josie. "Do you like dogs?" he asked.

"Doesn't everyone?" she answered, reaching for her latte, needing something to hold.

"No. And you're not allergic to them?"

"No."

"How do you feel about having a dog in the house?" he

asked.

"It's your house, Bear. You're the landlord. You make the rules."

"Now you're sounding a little prissy."

Josie leaned across the table, glaring into his eyes. "I am not. I'm being sincere. It's your house. You can do what you want."

"Then why are you angry?"

"It's just a lot, Bear, but give me a moment, and I'll catch up. I went from being all excited to have coffee with you to your ex is back, she's moved in, and you have a dog together."

"We don't have a dog together. It's not my dog. It's my friend Noah's."

Josie's heart suddenly plummeted, and all fight abruptly left her. "Noah was your friend that died in the pile up in Idaho."

Bear nodded.

She closed her eyes and bit her lip to hold back the sting of tears. Poor Bear. Poor Noah. "I'm glad you're going to take his dog," she said, opening her eyes, hoping he couldn't see the sheen of moisture. "What's his name?"

"Mick."

"Mick," Josie repeated.

"He's an Australian Shepherd. Very smart dog, high energy." Bear's forehead furrowed. "He's probably not going to love living in the house here in town."

"That's a complication, but we'll make it work. I can take Mick for walks in the morning and then again in the afternoon—"

"He's not your responsibility."

"But I want to help."

"You always do."

Josie winced a little, even as she knew Bear hadn't meant anything unkind by it. "I'm being pushy," she said. "I'm sorry."

"You're fine. I'm still trying to figure all of this out."

Frowning, she took a quick sip of her coffee. "So, there's more."

"There's Savannah."

Once again Josie's insides did that awful nauseating free fall. "Does she want to get back together with you?" she asked lowly.

He shook his head. "No. No, um, it's kind of hard to explain, but Noah and Savannah have been together for the past year. I don't know how serious they were—no, that's not true. Noah was very serious about Savannah, and I'm not sure what she felt, or how committed she was, but that's not the issue now."

"What is the issue?"

"Savannah's pregnant."

"Noah's baby?"

"Yes." Bear said.

"And now he's gone," Josie whispered.

"Yes."

"I understand now." She thought for a moment, and then carefully put her thoughts into words. "I might be missing something, though. Why doesn't Savannah want to keep their dog? I mean, if they were living together, wasn't it her dog, too?"

"She's not a big dog person. Or animal person. But that might be due to her lifestyle more than anything. She's a singer, and she's often traveling, and Noah usually took Mick with him when he went anywhere. They were inseparable. The only reason Mick wasn't on that trip to Pendleton is because he'd had an upset stomach. Crazy how a bout of diarrhea saved Mick's life."

"Mick's going to have a hard time without Noah then."

"He will. He's also going to find this change tough. He's used to being in the truck every day, going to the stables, being on the road."

"Too bad you've just leased out your ranch."

"No. That had to happen." Bear rubbed his bristled jaw, troubled. "It's going to be an adjustment, but we can do this."

Josie didn't know if the *we* was Bear and Mick, or Bear and her, or Bear, Josie and Mick, but it didn't matter. She was on team Anderson, and she'd do what she could to make the dog's—and Bear's—transition easier.

"Are you all moved in now?" Bear asked, changing the subject.

"I just have some books and things to bring over, but otherwise, I'm in."

"What do you think?"

"I think you have a great little house."

"Want to show me what you've done?"

"Not yet. You have to wait until I get the furniture in, and it's all being delivered tomorrow."

"Don't you need me there?"

"No. Rye said he'd stop by." She reached across the table and linked her fingers through his. "Can't wait for you to see it all, though. I just want you happy."

He glanced down at their hands and then back up into her eyes. "I'm happy," he said, voice pitched low and husky. "Happier than I ever thought I'd be again."

Don't cry. Don't cry. Whatever you do don't cry.

Josie contented herself with just giving his fingers a quick light squeeze, even though her heart felt impossibly full. She loved him.

Could he possibly love her? If not now, then one day?

Chapter Ten

MICK WASN'T SURE about Bear's wheelchair the first few days, but by the end of the week, he padded at Bear's side, or lay outside Bear's bedroom, waiting for him to go somewhere. He liked going on errands, and was always the first one outside, ready to hop in Bear's truck.

Savannah ... well, she was an entirely different matter. She, too, wanted to follow Bear around the house but he wasn't comfortable with her in the house or around him. He didn't dislike her—that much—but he hadn't forgiven her for betraying him. Breaking up with him was one thing. But ending her pregnancy? Getting rid of their baby without talking to him? Without him even being part of the conversation?

And the fact that she was pregnant again with Noah's child and behaving the exact same way blew his mind.

What was wrong with her? How selfish could she be?

So no, he wasn't happy Savannah was in his house, but he was gone tomorrow, which meant she'd be gone tomorrow.

He'd been reminding her daily that she needed a plan, and a place to go, but she was stalling, and he suspected she was still holding out for a chance to move with him to Marietta. That was most definitely not happening, but she didn't seem to believe him, which was her way of getting what she wanted.

Savannah nearly always got what she wanted.

On the plus side, the Cahill family from LA were leasing the house furnished which made it easy for him to leave tomorrow. Bear just needed to finish packing his clothes, toiletries and essentials. Most of his things were already shoved in duffel bags and a couple boxes, ready to be loaded into the back of his truck.

"The cleaning crew are coming in the morning at ten thirty," he told Savannah Thursday afternoon when she wandered into the kitchen in a barely there robe, which meant barely covered her assets, and her hair in a high messy ponytail. "You'll need to be completely out by the time they arrive. Is that going to be an issue?"

"Can't I get a later check out?" she asked, reaching into the refrigerator for a bottle of bubbly water.

"I've promised the cleaning service that the house will be theirs when their staff get here. That's the agreement."

"But why can't we be here while they're here? Couldn't they skip my room until the end? No hotel check in is until at least three o'clock."

Bear just stared at her.

She didn't flinch. "What am I supposed to do for five hours, Bear? Where do I go until then?"

"I didn't invite you to Montana."

"You're so cold."

"I have a lot going on. Maybe that's rude, but it's the truth. I can't take care of you. I can't babysit you. You're not my responsibility." He looked her in the eye and held her gaze. "You should call Noah's parents and tell them what's going on, and I know they'll help you. They'll be far more sympathetic to your situation than I am."

"And if I don't?"

He shrugged. "Then you're on your own."

He started to leave the kitchen, but Savannah stepped in front of him blocking his exit. "Will you let me talk to your roommate? The girl who isn't your girlfriend?" Savannah asked. "Can I introduce myself to her and see what she thinks? She might like me. She might not object ... not if you're both friends."

"I object. Isn't that enough?"

"I just need a bed. I need somewhere safe to sleep. That's all I want, all I need. Give me a week to figure out my next steps. I've been too down, too sad to think clearly." She hesitated, tears filling her eyes. "I miss Noah. I miss his calls. I miss his voice. I miss knowing someone loved me."

"Did you love him, Savannah?"

"I was growing to love him. He and I were different from you and me—"

"We don't need to go there."

"Just saying it was a different relationship."

Bear's jaw worked. "He adored you, and I didn't, right?"

Her slender shoulders twisted. "He put me first."

Whereas Bear hadn't. He exhaled slowly. "I'll ask Josie if she's open to meeting you, but if she isn't, you are on your own. And even if she does, that doesn't mean she'll want you in the house."

Savannah straightened, instantly on guard. "Why not? What did you tell her about me?"

"Nothing. But if she knew, she wouldn't think it's appropriate to have you in the house with us. I don't think it's appropriate, but Noah was a good friend of mine, and whatever I do for you is because of my loyalty to him." He reached out and used his arm to gently but firmly push her back so he could escape.

Twenty minutes later, Bear was still feeling trapped and restless, and he decided to head to Marietta and go to his house. It was his house after all, and he was moving in tomorrow so why not see it today?

Mick jumped into the truck, sitting in the passenger seat while Bear popped the tires off his wheelchair, loaded those behind him, and then leaned his seat back to put the frame over his shoulder in the backseat. Once the chair was in, and he was buckled up, he set off, glad to be getting away from the ranch—and Savannah.

The bottom line was that she couldn't move in to the Marietta house. But Savannah was not going to just go quietly into the night. She would hound him—and Josie—

until she had a definitive, negative answer from Josie.

Bear called Josie while driving.

"Tomorrow is the big day," she sang cheerfully as she answered his call.

"Can today be the big day?"

"You want to move in today?"

"No, but I'd love to see the house today if I could. It'd make me feel better about tomorrow."

"Oh, Bear, are you having regrets?"

"No regrets about buying the new house, or moving, but regrets about allowing Savannah to stay in Clyde Park for a few days."

"I wondered how that was going."

"Badly."

"I'm sorry."

"I don't want to put you in the middle."

"I'm not. Am I?"

He sighed, and ruffled his hair, dragging his hand through the short strands. "She wants to meet you. She thinks that once you meet her, you won't object to her staying with us for a week—or more."

Josie didn't answer, and Bear's stomach hurt. He was stressed and frustrated and torn between being a decent human being and saving his sanity.

"What do you want, Bear?" Josie asked carefully, quietly.

"I want her to go away." He felt like a child, and he hated it.

He hated feeling cornered. He resented that Savannah could make him feel guilty and responsible when he hadn't been part of her life for years.

"But I also don't want to drive her to desperation and then she just terminates this pregnancy like she's done before."

Again, Josie took her time answering. "Why do I feel like there's more to this story than you're telling me?"

"Because there is."

"Will you tell me?"

"Maybe. Someday." He sighed even as his chest tightened, squeezing, trapping the air in his lungs. "It's hard to talk about."

"She hurt you," Josie said.

"We hurt each other," he answered. "But she got the last word, and it did hurt. A lot."

"I'm sorry."

"It was a long time ago."

"Not that long ago, Bear. I thought it was three years ago this summer you were hurt, and at the time you two were engaged."

"Yes." He swallowed hard. "It'll be three years in September."

"So almost three years, and I can't imagine she broke up with you right away?"

He sighed again, increasingly unsettled. "This isn't my favorite subject."

"I think my point is that she's not part of a distant past. Savannah has only been out of your life for a year or two." Josie paused before pressing on. "And it sounds as if she wants back into your life."

"That's not going to happen," he growled.

"It's already happened," Josie answered before adding, "I'm happy to meet her. Just let me know when and where."

Silence stretched across the line, and Bear felt ridiculous. He felt awkward and immature and emotional. He hated involving Josie in his problems. She shouldn't have to deal with Savannah. He should be able to deal with Savannah. If he were a real man—

"Josie," he said roughly, "you don't have to show me the house today. I can wait until tomorrow. I imagine you're doing a lot of last-minute things."

"I am, but it's okay."

"No. It's not. We have a plan, and we're going to stick to the plan. I'll see you tomorrow."

Hanging up, Bear pulled off to the side of the road, texted Savannah that she wouldn't be meeting with Josie, and she wouldn't be staying at the Marietta house, and there would be no more discussion on it, or delaying her departure from Clyde Park either.

Bear sat in his truck for what seemed like hours, just looking at the mountains he loved, and the place that had been his second home. His dad's job meant that they moved every couple of years, but this place, this land was always here and, despite all the changes Bear had known, especially in the last few years, it felt immensely reassuring to see that not everything had changed. The undulating land, rolling up into the Crazies, the sweeping sky overhead, the fat white clouds slowly sailing past.

He couldn't sell this place—this was his legacy—but he couldn't be here now. Bear's gaze swept the miles of pasture, the fields that did well when planted, fields that hadn't been consistently planted since his grandfather died.

He could live here one day, be here one day, but not yet. He wasn't ready. He needed to get his business started, needed to work on developing his business model, making it successful so it'd be possible for others to follow.

If he'd had kids, this would be something he'd pass to them, but perhaps one of Susie's children might want to be here, perhaps one of the boys or girls might want to make Montana home. If that was the case, he'd make sure the land was worth having, that he'd taken care of it the same way he would for his own.

Bear would reach out to his neighbor who'd leased the land for the past four years and see if he wanted to extend the agreement. And if he didn't want to, Bear would speak to others. He wasn't worried. If there was anything he'd learned from his accident, it was that life was far more fluid than he'd understood. Life wasn't just one thing, one moment, one dream. His world may have changed, but the world was still there, still ripe with energy and opportunity. He just had to take it.

JOSIE WAS STANDING on the sidewalk of the Marietta house overseeing the delivery of Bear's new furniture when a black Mercedes SUV pulled up in front of the house, squeezing in front of the furniture truck.

Josie tried to remember if she was expecting anyone else today. She was to meet a woman from the blind company, but that wasn't supposed to be this afternoon. The curtains were already up—Josie had made those herself—but she'd ordered blinds that could be controlled by a remote at the last moment, realizing Bear would want them for easy control of light and privacy in his bedroom, bathroom, and living room.

But as a tall, slender blonde stepped from the Mercedes, flipping thick sun-streaked hair over her shoulder, Josie dismissed the idea that this was a woman who worked with a discount manufacturer.

This was Savannah. Had to be Bear's Savannah.

Josie crossed the sidewalk and walked to the curb to meet her. "Savannah?"

The stunning blond looked her up and down. "Josie?"

"Yes."

Savannah's brown gaze narrowed. "You're smaller than I expected."

Josie shrugged. "Don't worry, I have plenty of attitude." She was tempted to cross her arms over her chest but didn't want to look defensive. "Bear's not here, in case you're looking for him."

"No, I'm not. I came to see you."

Josie could feel Savannah's continued scrutiny. It was strange to have another woman study her so intently. "I'd invite you in but it's pretty chaotic. That's why I'm staying out here. I don't want to get in everyone's way."

Savannah finally looked away, her gaze now on the square plain house. "This is Bear's house?" she asked in disbelief.

"Yes."

"Wow. He's certainly come down in the world."

Chin up, Josie held her tongue. She was not going to get into it with Savannah of all people.

Savannah focused back on Josie. "Do you know about his new business?"

"I do."

"And you support it?"

"I think it's exciting. Don't you?"

For a minute, Savannah didn't answer and then her expression shifted, awareness dawning. "This isn't about helping paralyzed people walk again, is it?"

"I'm sorry?" Josie said coldly. She was struggling to keep her temper in check.

"A couple years ago, after his friend was hurt, Bear had

this idea that people could walk again if they were covered in braces from head to foot—"

"Those are real, and they're called exoskeletons," Josie said, feeling a funny twitch behind her eyes.

"Yes, they're oh so wonderful, but it didn't save his friend. Sean still died."

"His bull rider friend?"

"Sean O'Leary, yes. He couldn't cope with his accident and took his life. So no, I'm not a fan of Bear's business venture. The freakish robotic suit didn't help Sean. Have you seen one? Looks like something from outer space. No one will benefit, not enough for Bear to sink all his money into this business."

"You're wrong. It will make a difference," Josie said fiercely. "I've done the research, and I've read what the doctors and therapists say. Getting spinal cord injured people on their feet and moving is so important—beneficial for the body and the mind."

"Have you ever seen Bear use one?"

"No."

"I have." Savannah stalked towards her, mockery gone, voice cracking. "What Bear did wasn't *walking*. The walker did the walking. Bear was just hanging on for the ride."

"Good for Bear—"

"Not good. Bad. You don't get it. You're not paying attention."

Josie pressed her lips tightly together as she met Savannah's gaze.

Savannah might be tough, but Josie was tough, too. "No, you're not paying attention, Savannah. Bear isn't sitting around gazing at his navel. He's not dwelling on what happened to him. He's using his accident to help others, and you should be proud of him. I am."

"Instead of encouraging Bear in his pursuit of altruism, something that could easily bankrupt him, why don't you encourage him to settle down, and accept who he is now, and what he can do now, and it isn't *walking*. Or riding. Or any of the other stuff he used to do."

"I'm so glad he's not living to please you but investing in others. He's going to make the world a better place."

"You mean he's just blowing his money."

Josie laughed. It was that or throw a punch at Savannah, and she hadn't thrown a punch at a girl since she and Hannah got into it in their teenage years. "I need to get back to work. Hope you have a nice life." Josie turned away and headed for the front steps.

"Are you guys together?" Savannah called out.

Josie froze.

"Are you seeing each other? Dating? Whatever you want to call it?" Savannah's voice was loud and brittle. "It's okay to tell me the truth. I just want to know."

Josie turned around. "What did Bear tell you?"

"He said you're just friends."

"The same thing I said." Josie's chin jerked up. "Satisfied

now?"

"You do know that Bear can't … get it up. So, there is that."

Josie blinked, shocked by Savannah's callousness. She'd suspected Bear's spinal cord injury might have impacted his ability to have sex, but it horrified her that Savannah felt comfortable tossing Bear's private information around as if playing a game of poppycock. "I wish I knew what Bear saw in you. Because all I see is a selfish, hard, cynical woman who doesn't like anyone else, probably because she doesn't like herself."

"I'm allowed to have opinions. Bear and I were together five years, two of those we were engaged. You've only just met him this summer."

"That may be the case, but you're not in relationship with him anymore, which means you should respect his privacy. With your long history together, I'd think you'd want to protect him, not expose him to scorn."

"I wasn't mocking him. Just stating facts."

"About his sexuality." Josie's voice hardened. She was going to lose her cool any moment. "That's not something that should be discussed, and I hate that you just spilled something so private and personal. Makes me think it's not the first time you spoke so carelessly—"

"You're serious? You're really upset."

"Yes."

"But if you're just friends?'

"Friends protect friends, Savannah." Josie's upper lip curled in disgust. "I'm glad we had the chance to meet because it made me realize this little house will never, ever be big enough for the three of us." And with that Josie swiftly walked away.

FRIDAY MORNING, BEAR had a surprise meeting with two executives from RobExStar. He'd reached out to them weeks ago and hadn't heard anything back, but suddenly two of the upper management were here in Marietta, working in a meeting with him on their way to a private, posh Yellowstone resort for the very wealthy and elite.

But the men were interested in Bear's business model and wanted to see his facility—which he was more than happy to show them. Rye had met Bear at the Farrell Building a half hour before the RobExStar's management team arrived and offered to take Mick so that Bear could focus on the executives.

Rye's suggestion was a good one, and Bear was grateful that Mick ran to Rye's truck and jumped in, giving Bear a few minutes to gather his thoughts. The two executives arrived right at nine, and Bear walked them through the empty, clean Farrell Building, explaining how his facility would work, and equipment needed to get the business off the ground. By the end of the hour, the executives were on board, promising to provide a number of needed exoskeletons to get the Marietta facility functioning, with a promise that if Marietta performed, they'd back the next city.

Bear was elated. It was huge getting RobExStar's support. Not having to purchase the first dozen exoskeletons meant he could keep the cost down for members, and he'd certainly gain some media coverage, too. He personally wasn't looking to franchise his idea, but Bear did hope others would get involved and do something similar in their communities. Until spinal cord injuries were a thing of the past, there had to be better treatments and options to extend and improve the quality of life for those with SCI.

It was a short drive from the Farrell Building to his house, and when Bear pulled up in his driveway there was no sign of a moving truck, or boxes, or anything indicating that the house was ready for him.

Bear rolled up the ramp on the side of the house and was just about to open the front door when Josie flung it open. "How did the meeting go?" she asked standing in front of him blocking his view.

"Great. Couldn't have gone better."

Josie gave him an impulsive hug. "That's fantastic. I'm so happy for you." She straightened, her cheeks slightly pink. "Want to see inside?"

"I do."

"Well, come in, or as they say on those TV shows, welcome home, Anderson Family. Welcome home." Smiling, she stepped back so that he could enter.

Bear's jaw dropped as he rolled into the house.

The house wasn't just furnished with the new furniture Josie had suggested, but it looked polished and masculine. Luxurious and beautiful.

His new furniture—the oversized leather sectional in a soft butterscotch leather—was flanked by end tables and a deep leather recliner studded with western nail heads. Stylish lamps were on the end tables, and they turned on and off with just a touch of his hand, or by a switch on the wall.

Josie had painted the walls a dark, rich chocolate, and the wide planks of the hardwood floor had been refinished. Because of his wheelchair there were no rugs, but she'd added woven textured pillows to the oversized couch, and plush chocolate drapes framed the tall windows.

"When did you do all this?" he asked.

"The last week or so," she said. "With a little help from Rye's crew. Ricco came over one evening to do the floors, and Rye and Ansley helped me paint."

"This doesn't look like the same house. It's … nice."

"Paint is a miracle worker. And next spring, I'd suggest new windows but that's for another time."

Bear did a slow circle, taking it all in. "I would never have thought to paint a small room a dark color, but it works."

"You have tall windows, and they let in so much light it washed out the room. I thought you'd enjoy a more masculine space, and you'll see that at night it glows. You'll never want to go out."

"Good. Because I don't like going out." He laughed, before moving on to the dining room, painted with the same dark chocolate paint, which worked as the two rooms opened into each other.

He touched the round pedestal dining table, thinking it was the perfect height for him to roll under. A thick slab of stone topped a sideboard that was slightly lower than expected. He recognized his teak dining table, but he hadn't bought the sideboard. "Where did this come from?" he asked.

"I found that in a thrift store here in town. I cut the legs down—"

"You did?"

She nodded, clearly proud. "I have my own saw and tools now. But I didn't cut the granite. The tile guys did that for me, and I think it looks really good. It's practical, too, as you can turn this into a buffet, and put hot and cold dishes on it without worrying about burning the wood."

"And since this is granite not marble, it can handle the heat, too," he said.

"Exactly."

"I'm really pleased."

"There is so much more. The kitchen, your bedroom and bathroom, the office. It's all done with you and your needs in mind—"

"I hope I'm not that demanding."

"No. And I went up and beyond in some cases since this is also for my project. I'm glad most of the interior is done, because Monday the Farrell Building is yours and I know we're going to be busy with that for a couple months. Are you still hoping for an October open date?"

"Rye thinks it's a little ambitious," Bear admitted. "He thinks November is a better bet, maybe even the new year since the weather will be a challenge."

"The weather is always a challenge. Tell my brother he has sixty to ninety days, and that's it. The work is mostly constructing your office, a break room, and the bathrooms."

"Which means just carpentry, plumbing, electrical, drywall, tile, painters, equipment."

She laughed. "See? Minor."

"When I first met Rye, I envied him for having such a positive working relationship with you. Now I feel for him. You're a task master."

"I am. But that's how we get stuff done around here."

"Speaking of around here, I hope you put some TLC into your own space."

"Come see," she invited, leading the way down the hall to her room.

Bear rolled just inside her door and glanced around. He was surprised at the simplicity. One wall had weathered boards from the ceiling to the floor, and the other three walls were a creamy white. Her bedframe was a dark gray metal. A vintage yellow and white sunburst quilt covered the bed. She had a small dresser with an oval mirror hanging above it while black and white framed photos of her family hung on another wall.

She sat down on the foot of her bed. "What do you think?"

"I think you should be a designer."

Josie grinned. "I had fun with this. It's a small room so I added a lot of textures—the reclaimed lumber for an accent wall, the metal bed frame, the quilt, the Queen Anne wall mirror."

"Did Rye do that wall for you?"

"I did it myself. He's shown me in the past how to use a power saw, so it was just a matter of measuring, cutting and attaching. Easy with a nail gun."

"You have skills."

"I have to. I can't afford to pay everyone to come in and execute my ideas. I have to be able to do a lot of it myself."

"So how would you describe your style? It's not that shabby chic look because this is very uncluttered."

"I'd say I'm a little farmhouse, a little eclectic. I can't handle clutter—maybe it's because my house growing up was full of things, and not very well organized—so I like to keep things simple. Clean lines."

Bear rolled further into her room, his attention on the framed photos. "That has to be you and your sister," he said, gesturing to a picture of two little girls outside, in matching dresses, smiling bravely even as they squinted against the sun. "How old were you here?"

"I had to be eight maybe? Hannah would have been maybe ten. We're fourteen months apart. If you ever see more photos of us, you'll discover that Mom almost always dressed us alike."

"Maybe it was the easiest."

"Maybe. But neither Hannah nor I liked it. We were very different as kids. Fought like cats and dogs."

"And that's your mom," he said, intently studying a photo of Jennifer Calhoun holding a baby with toddlers at her side.

"Yes, that's Mom holding Jasper after he finally got to come home from the hospital. And then of course that's Hannah and me. I don't know where Rye was."

"Maybe he was the one taking the picture. He would have been old enough."

"I bet you're right."

"You do look like your mom," Bear said. "It's rather amazing. You both have the same long dark hair, purple-blue eyes … and those cheekbones."

"Hannah has the same cheekbones, just different color eyes."

"Different face shape, too. She has a more angular jaw."

"She has Rye's jaw. She's lucky. I always envied her a little bit. I wanted to look more like her."

"You're beautiful."

Josie shook her head. "Don't say that."

"It's true."

Her cheeks grew rosier. "I wasn't fishing for compliments." She jumped to her feet. "Let's go check out your office and bedroom, and then I'll help you bring your things in from the truck." She suddenly paused, glanced outside and then back to Bear. "Where is the dog? I thought Mick was coming with you."

"Rye has him. He offered to take him while I had my meeting and got settled in here. Mick was wildly enthusiastic, too. He couldn't wait to leap into Rye's truck."

"Rye loves dogs."

"I do, too, but Mick isn't bonding with me the way I'd hoped."

"Maybe the wheelchair makes him skittish?"

"Or maybe he just likes Rye better."

Josie didn't know if Bear was hurt by the defection or not. "He's been through a lot of change. Maybe Rye reminds him of Noah."

"Maybe."

"Does it bother you?" she asked.

Bear hesitated and then shook his head. "No, it's actually a relief. Mick needs a lot of room to run, and I don't have it here, not in town." Bear looked sheepish. "I'm trying not to take it personally, but Mick seems to prefer Rye over me."

Josie was trying not to smile. "It might just be that, um, dogs love Rye."

"Your brother is saving the day. I just want Mick happy, and if Mick is happiest with Rye, then I'm good. It's what Noah would want anyway."

Chapter Eleven

SUNDAY NIGHT, BEAR organized a dinner at his new house and invited Rye and Ansley to join them. He also invited Cormac Sheenan and his wife Whitney, but they already had plans with friends and took a raincheck, promising to have them over soon.

Josie set the dining room table for four and put together a small centerpiece from some of the scraggly rose bushes and overgrown perennials in the backyard. But with dimmed lighting and small votive candles on the table, everything looked quite nice, and Josie couldn't wait for Ansley to see how much Bear's house had changed. It was funny how this wasn't her house, but it kind of was. She'd poured herself into the renovations, even though they were small, picking out tiles for his bathroom that she thought he'd like, as well as finishes that would be rich and textured, making his home feel bigger and more luxurious than it might have been otherwise.

Two hours before Rye and Ansley were to arrive, Ansley phoned Josie and asked if it would be okay if they brought a couple of guests.

"Anyone I know?" Josie asked, wondering if it was perhaps Lachlan or another one of Ansley's brothers.

"One guess."

"Your brother."

"No. He's four legged and has a great black and white coat."

Josie laughed. "Yes, bring Mick, of course. Bear will be happy to see him."

"Are you sure that Bear really is okay that Mick has adopted us?"

"We just discussed this and Bear is happy that Mick is happy. He said it's what Noah would want. But now you have me curious. Is Mick bringing a date?"

"Depends on your definition of date. It's Savannah—"

"*No.*" Josie's tone was flat and firm. "I can't deal with her again."

"She's been staying with us for the weekend. I've been helping her find a place to live."

"Tell her to go back to Nashville."

"She's left Nashville, Josie." Ansley fell silent and the silence wasn't the most comfortable. "She's sorry for dropping in on you like that, and the things she said."

"She can just send me an apology by text. That will be fine."

"Josie."

"Ansley, she's not a nice person. You should have heard the things she said about Bear. She can say what she wants about me—I'm a Calhoun and tough, I've heard it all—but

Bear doesn't deserve her scorn. Bear deserves respect."

"And Savannah deserves compassion. She hasn't exactly had it easy. Think about it from her perspective for a moment. She'd been madly in love with Bear, and he's injured in the arena and almost died. He spends months in the hospital—"

"I know all of this."

"Let me finish." Ansley drew a quick breath. "Even though they try, they can't make it work, and a year after his accident they both move on. Less than two years after, she's now in love again and her partner is killed in one of the worst freeway pile ups in recent history. Worse, she's pregnant and between the grief and all her hormones, she can't even see straight. I'm not asking you to be buddies with her but let her come for dinner and at least listen to what she has to say."

Josie chewed on the inside of her cheek, fighting her frustration, fighting resentment. Who was Ansley to tell her how to behave? And yet Josie adored her sister-in-law and respected her immensely. "Bear doesn't know she came by. He has no idea we've met."

"Tell him then."

"I don't even know how she found out where we lived."

"Savannah told me she'd saw his forwarding address in the mail. The post office sent a confirmation, and she wrote it down."

"So, she's a snoop and a bully," Josie said dryly.

"Are you really saying she can't come?"

Josie sighed and flopped back on her bed. "You owe me."

"What do you want?"

"I want an Ansley Art original. Nothing big, just something small, eight by ten or nine by nine. Something I can hang in my room, or put on my nightstand, and every time I look at it I can think how lucky you are to have me for a sister."

Ansley laughed, and then Josie was laughing.

"Deal," Ansley said. "But you need to break the news to Bear that Savannah will be joining us—just for the evening, and not to be dropping by again…at least, not unless she's invited. That's coming from her, too. She said it's a promise."

"Fine. Bring her tonight. I'll see you all later."

Josie left her bedroom and went searching for Bear who she'd thought was watching a baseball game in the living room, but instead had returned to his office, and was typing away at his laptop, which had been attached to a docking station featuring an enormous screen.

She lightly knocked on his partially open door.

"Josie, you don't have to knock," he called to her "Come in."

She pushed the door open and leaned against the doorway, happy to see how happy he was at his new desk. He loved the screen, as well as the sound system attached. She'd heard him play games late at night and it made her feel good that he had something to do when he couldn't sleep. She wondered if he was up so late because he hurt or if his brain just wouldn't shut off.

"I just had a call from Ansley," Josie said.

"They're not cancelling, are they?" Bear asked, looking up from his keyboard.

"No. But they'd like to bring a guest."

"That's not a problem."

She couldn't help making a face. "It's Savannah."

"*What?*"

She crossed to the refurbished armchair facing his desk to sit down. "Did you know Savannah's been staying with them?"

"No." He sat back in his chair and rubbed his face. "But then I was frustrated with Savannah for not leaving the house Friday morning—she was hiding in an upstairs bedroom and wouldn't come down—and I told Rye I'd had it with her. He said he'd get her out. I didn't know that meant he'd move her into his house."

Josie deliberated about telling Bear that Savannah had dropped by Thursday and said awful things and then decided it wouldn't help—any of them. "If you don't want her here tonight, I'll call Ansley back."

"I don't really care as long as she leaves with Rye and Ansley."

"I agree with you there." She looked into Bear's face, admiring his lovely, rugged features and silver-gray eyes. "I'm sorry my family got involved."

"I got your brother involved. That's on me."

"I'll add another setting to the table," Josie said, rising. "And no matter what happens, we'll survive." She paused in the doorway and glanced back at him. "And they're bringing Mick. I didn't think you'd mind if he came."

"No, Mick is always welcome here."

"I thought so."

Rye, Ansley, Savannah, and a very energetic Mick arrived at precisely six. Bear already had the grill going and the steaks seasoned. They were doing a simple summer dinner with steak, baked potatoes, green salad, watermelon, and huckleberry crisp for dessert.

Bear and Rye disappeared to the small backyard—a place that wasn't fixed up yet, but it had a cement patio which worked for Bear—and Josie was in the kitchen checking on the baked potatoes. Ansley had brought the salad and watermelon, and Josie had made the Calhoun family's berry crisp earlier, remembering that Rye had once said he loved berry cobblers and crisps.

Savannah was quiet but also polite during the dinner. It struck Josie that Savannah was being on her very best behavior, and Josie didn't know if it was to impress Ansley and Rye, or if the South Carolina native was truly remorseful for her rude behavior Thursday.

Once, during dinner, Bear caught Josie's eye and he gave her a look that made her think he understood exactly what she was thinking. She gave him a faint smile, grateful that he got her.

It was after dinner, and everyone had gone to the living room to relax while Josie dished up the berry crisp and added a scoop of ice cream.

Suddenly, Savannah appeared, carrying empty glasses. "Where should I put these?" she asked.

"Next to the sink," Josie answered.

Savannah set them down but then hesitated. "Is there anything I can do to help?"

Josie smiled tightly. "I've got it but thank you."

Still, Savannah hesitated, hovering in front of the dining room doorway. "I owe you an apology," she said unsteadily. "I behaved badly Thursday when I stopped by. I was rude, and I did say things that were unforgiveable. I'm sorry. I'm sorry for what I said, and I'm sorry I said it to you. I've been having a really difficult time and—" She broke off, lips pressing together, throat aching. It took her a long moment to continue. "But it doesn't make it right. The truth is…" She gulped a breath. "I kind of hate myself, and you're so nice—"

"I'm not that nice."

"No, you are. Much nicer than me."

"I don't find it hard to be nice."

"I do." Savannah grimaced. "Being nice is so difficult. Makes me want to throw up a little bit. Not everywhere. Just in my mouth."

Josie nearly smiled, but she suppressed it. Savannah was so ridiculous and yet there was also something … something … about her. "I accept your apology, but, Savannah, I think it's highly unlikely we're going to be friends.

"I get that, and totally respect that. It might not surprise you, but I don't have a lot of friends. Women don't love me. Or even like me very much."

Josie gave her a pointed look. "Maybe if you were nicer?"

Savannah winced. "I deserve that."

Josie set the large serving spoon down. "I'm going to be honest. I'm not sure how I feel about you staying at my brother's house. Is that a long-term thing, or…"

Savannah flushed. "Your brother and Ansley have been really good to me."

"They're good people."

"Ansley has been helping me find a place and tomorrow I'm going with her to her brother's in Paradise Valley. He's living on the Campbell family ranch—"

"You're going to move in with Lachlan?" Josie asked incredulously.

"I don't remember his name. She has a lot of brothers. But whoever is living there has to return to Texas for a little bit, and I'm supposed to keep an eye on the house and her uncle." Savannah must have seen Josie's stricken expression because she hastily added. "The uncle has professional caregivers. I'm not doing nursing duty. Ansley thought it would be good for me to be there as back up."

"Are you going to be okay in such a remote place? There's no one around except for the Wyatts, and they're pretty busy with their own family."

Savannah shrugged. "I'm getting paid. It's basically a house-sitting job and that's better than nothing."

Josie returned to dishing up the last two crisps. "Bear told me you had an entire summer of concerts lined up. Big shows every weekend and smaller venues midweek."

"They're not glamorous."

"Most work isn't glamorous." Josie took in the shadows beneath Savannah's eyes and the sadness in her gaze. Savannah wasn't as tough as she sounded. If anything, she was pretty much a mess. "And I'd think that constantly traveling and performing is grueling, no matter the size of the audience."

"True." Savannah's mouth quirked. "Which is why I'm happy to make a little money staying put. A couple weeks house sitting in the mountains sounds pretty ideal to me."

Chapter Twelve

WITH SAVANNAH SETTLED a thirty-minute drive from Marietta on the Campbell's Cold Canyon Ranch for the next couple of weeks, Josie finally began to relax and enjoy the house and what was left of her summer. Happily, it was proving to be the best summer she could remember.

There was so much to do in Marietta and she and Bear enjoyed checking out all the restaurants and bars and weekend farmer's markets. On the nights that Josie didn't work at Ansley's gallery, she and Bear would hang out, or go do something fun, whether it was a movie, or a meal, or to listen to music in Bozeman. They always went Dutch, because Josie valued her independence, and Bear was not responsible for her. He was her friend, and she was determined to be a good friend to him, which meant keeping a tight rein on her emotions, and her deepening feelings, as well as her attachment to him.

She loved working at the gallery. Josie was good at it, too, and sold more pieces than Ansley did, probably because she had no self-consciousness about discussing Ansley's talent. Ansley was extraordinary, young, and would be a huge name one day. Her work was an investment and collectors would be wise to buy her pieces now, while they were relatively affordable.

Josie met a lot of tourists working at the gallery, but then there were the locals and serious art collectors who traveled to Marietta just to see Ansley's work. Some shoppers wanted Josie's opinion—which painting would look best in a particular room—while others wanted nothing from her, making it very clear that they were merely looking and didn't need any assistance.

Bear would often pop in on Thursday nights, since it was the one night during the work week that the gallery stayed open until ten o'clock. He'd bring her an iced tea or a snack and would stay and visit if there was no one in the gallery. If she was busy, he'd leave the treat for her behind the elegant little counter and look around the gallery before leaving.

Tonight, he didn't rush away despite the gallery having several different groups of people shopping. As she answered questions one couple had about Ansley's work, Josie watched Bear from the corner of her eye. He was slowly rolling around the exhibit, spending most of his time in front of the Montana landscapes. She also loved the Montana mountains and valleys, as well as the paintings featuring the various rivers in all of Montana's seasons.

She was glad Bear was lingering. She liked having him here. He always made her feel safe and protected. She also found comfort in his company, even if they weren't speaking. Josie secretly hoped that Bear would stay longer. They'd both been busy this week and hadn't spent as much time together as they had.

BEAR HAD SWUNG by the gallery tonight to say hello to Josie, and then he was going to leave and try to get some reading done at home. But once he entered the gallery, Bear had no desire to go. He felt restless tonight, a little bored, a little irritable and he suspected it had to do with not seeing much of Josie this week.

He missed her. He missed talking and making her laugh. He missed her lovely face and those eyes that crinkled at the corners when she smiled. Tonight, she wore a simple lilac summer dress. It was fitted but had classic lines, and with her long, dark hair and stunning eyes she took his breath away. There was a part of him that thought of her as his—his girl, his woman, his heart—but at the same time, it wasn't realistic, and he did his best to tamp down the thoughts and all the frustrating emotions.

He admired her work ethic. Josie was always busy, always coming and going, always working on something. But this week, he'd really missed talking with her, hanging out with her, watching shows with her. He missed morning coffee with her. Missed sipping her weird golden ginger turmeric good-for-you drink that she made in the evening for them. He missed her telling him how important magnesium was and counting out three magnesium gummies for him to take before bed.

It was strange that he couldn't remember actually missing anyone before—other than his family. He'd loved Savannah but never really missed her. They were both so busy, and always traveling, and they never had a lot to talk about. Their reunions were generally wordless, too, reconnecting through sex. Lots of sex.

The last time he'd had sex was a few days before his accident. Savannah had flown in to Tulsa for a night, a quick visit between concerts, and they did what they did best—hot, fierce lovemaking that left them both spent and content.

Savannah always physically satisfied him. He'd never considered hooking up with anyone once he was committed to Savannah, but after he was hurt, after sex was the one thing he couldn't do with her, they didn't know how to communicate. They didn't seem to have anything to say to each other. The silences were brutal and full of frustration and resentment.

She resented him for getting hurt and changing.

He resented her for missing who he'd been. It was bad enough grieving for his loss of sensation and loss of control without her so deeply unhappy that he was now *paralyzed.*

Sometimes, she masked her horror, but other times she couldn't, her unhappiness building up in her until she blew, venting all of her rage and misery. That was how he'd discovered she'd been pregnant when he was hurt. And that was how he'd discovered she'd gotten rid of the baby.

He'd forgiven her—more or less—but he hadn't forgotten. Despite his life on the road, despite the rigors of his sport, he was a family man, and looked forward to the day he'd have a wife and children.

Now Bear wondered why he'd thought Savannah would make a great wife and mother, but at the time, he'd been fooled by her Southern girl charm, and her Carolina accent, and her long, golden hair, her big brown eyes, and her legs that were a mile long.

He fell for the package and didn't look deeper. Fool that he was.

Thank God, Josie was nothing like Savannah. Josie was unlike anyone else.

Bear parked himself in front of the wall featuring the new smaller Ansley works. They were elegantly framed and all featured barns and farmhouses, fenced pastures and creeks, and even one was Paradise Valley's historic one room schoolhouse.

Finally, the people Josie had been talking to left the gallery, wandering out right after the other couple, and she crossed the gallery to give Bear a hug.

"You don't usually stay," she said, straightening.

She smelled sweet and fresh, like lemon blossoms, or was it that lemon myrtle body wash from the box of scented bath products Susie had sent him as a housewarming gift? Bear wasn't about to use lemon blossom anything on his body, so he'd given those bath products to her, and kept the eucalyptus ones for himself. "You smell good," he said.

"It's the stuff your sister sent you. I love it."

"I'll have her send some more."

"No, don't do that. I saw how expensive the shipping was to get that box here. It was forty-eight dollars."

"Australian," he said. He gestured to the wall with the seven framed paintings.

"I like these. When did Ansley complete them?"

"Just recently. She brought three in last weekend, and then four new ones a few days ago."

"She doesn't typically do a lot of buildings," Bear said, seeing that two of the seven framed pieces already had red dots on the price, indicating they'd sold. Fortunately, the Paradise Valley school house, the one he was most interested in, was still available.

"Only if there was a barn or something on the horizon, but never anything quite this intimate. I like them," Josie answered. "They're a bit dreamy. Not quite impressionistic, but I feel like there is a timelessness to them, a sense of nostalgia."

"As if you've been there, or you'd like to be there," he said.

"Yes, exactly." She smiled happily at him. "We are so much alike it's scary."

"Twins."

She laughed out loud, her lovely eyes filled with light and

warmth. "It's so good to have you here. I've missed you."

"You were busy this week."

"I've picked up a client," Josie said. "Cormac's wife asked if she could hire me to refresh their cottage at Flathead Lake. We're not going to start the work until summer ends, but we've begun looking at paint and fabric and some new furniture."

"This is great. When did it happen?"

"We met Monday for coffee, and she hired me then. Tuesday, we went through the magazine clippings she'd saved, and then Wednesday I shared some of my ideas. She's lovely, you know." Ansley leaned toward him to whisper. "And she wants to commission Ansley to do an original of Flathead Lake and the Mission Mountains, which would be the centerpiece for the cottage living room."

"Cormac doesn't strike me as a cottage kind of guy," Bear said.

"I think they use the word cottage loosely. Their place is two or three stories and has over sixty-five hundred square feet."

"I get it now. But good for you, and good for Ansley. You two make quite the design team."

"*And* we do have Rye in our back pocket." She flexed her lean but impressive bicep. "Calhoun and Campbell power."

"You are so goofy," he said.

"I know. But it's good. It's far better than taking oneself too seriously."

"I agree." Bear turned and faced the gallery wall. "If it's still available, I want this schoolhouse."

"Really? Why?"

He shrugged. "My dad grew up attending school in a one room schoolhouse, the Benton Lake School, a half hour north of Great Falls, and it makes me think of him. He went there from kindergarten until he was fourteen."

"There's not much north of Great Falls."

"Farms. Ranches. My dad grew up in a farming family."

"And your mom's dad was a rancher."

Bear nodded, bittersweet emotion filling him. He hadn't felt much of anything positive for so long and now he was feeling good things again, feelings that weren't dark and heavy, feelings that weren't despair. The newness of these emotions staggered him. He'd doubted he'd ever again feel warmth and tenderness, joy and gratitude. Or love. But he felt love.

Love for his parents who had been truly good people.

Love for his sister, who had rushed to his side when he was hurt, and then stayed with him for months until he was stable.

Love for beautiful, passionate Josie Calhoun, whom he couldn't have, but that didn't mean he couldn't appreciate her, and love her from afar.

"Where did your dad go to school when he turned fourteen?" Josie asked.

"My grandmother homeschooled him for a year, and

then once he had his license, he drove himself to high school in Great Falls. He was, by all accounts, quite the athlete—a good quarterback and a great pitcher."

"Did you play sports in school?"

"I did."

"I imagine you were a good athlete, too."

"I was," he said modestly.

Josie laughed, and the sound of her laughing made him laugh.

"How did your parents meet?" she asked.

"Hiking. Mom loved being out of doors, and Dad was a brand-new park ranger and they met on a trail. He saw she was alone and mentioned that there had been an aggressive moose in the area and to be careful."

"And they fell in love and lived happily ever after?"

"Not exactly. He fell for her, but she wasn't interested in being anyone's girlfriend. She liked her independence and my dad, although well-meaning, was always trying to help her."

Josie grinned. "And she didn't want or need his help."

"Exactly."

"How long did it take him to convince her he was the one?"

"Almost three years."

"He was persistent."

"Had to be. Mom had a stubborn streak, but once she fell for him, she fell hard and after all those years of courtship, they married quickly, after just a few weeks."

"They were happy together?"

"Very. From the time they married, they spent very little time apart."

She knew his parents were both gone, but she didn't know when or how they'd died and wasn't comfortable asking. "When is the last time you saw your sister?"

"Christmas, eighteen months ago." Bear frowned. "I can't believe it's already been that long."

"Go see her."

"In Australia?"

"Why not? Buy a first class or business seat, stretch out, watch a couple movies, get some sleep and arrive rested."

"You make it sound easy. It's a long trip."

"Yes, but this is your sister, and you miss her." Josie glanced at the gold framed painting of the schoolhouse on the wall. "If you want it, I'll ring you up, but I think Ansley is trying to keep the grouping through the weekend. She'll have new pieces next week to replace the sold ones."

"That's fine. Just bring my painting home when Ansley gives the okay."

SATURDAY, JOSIE DIDN'T have to be at the gallery until noon and was enjoying a slow morning at the house. Bear made them a late breakfast of scrambled eggs, country-fried potatoes, sausage, and toast. Josie wasn't a big fan of sausage, so she let Bear have hers, but she'd enjoyed sitting in the booth sketching some ideas for the front of his house while keeping an eye on him while he cooked. It was obvious he knew how to make eggs, and his country-style potatoes were perfectly crispy with just the right amount of seasoning.

They ate at the kitchen table and after he'd finished clearing his plate, he asked her what she was working on.

"Just some sketches of your house, and what it could look like." She looked at him. "You do know you have to do something to the exterior. Your house has no curb appeal. It's rather embarrassing, and not fit for a Montana legend."

"You can let go of the legend stuff now, Josie Calhoun. I'm not much of a legend."

"Sure you are. Not only did you survive a grizzly attack, but you survived being thrown *and* stomped on by one of the rankest bulls in the history of the sport. I'm not into rodeos and bull riding but even I know that's pretty impressive."

"You really enjoy giving me grief."

"I certainly enjoy playing with you—" She blushed furiously the moment the words left her mouth. "Because it's fun teasing you." She frowned. "Nothing is coming out right."

Bear grinned, his expression devilish but thoughtfully didn't add to her embarrassment. "What would you do to the exterior if you could?"

"First, I'd replace the windows. These vinyl windows are an eyesore. And then I'd give you a great looking front porch." She turned the sketchbook around so he could see, and she showed him the drawing. "I'd add some proper columns for craftsman style. Some shingles here. Some siding there. With the windows, I'd add narrow planter boxes beneath for color and texture. What do you think?"

He studied it a moment before giving her a rueful look. "I think that's a lot of money."

"We could skip the planter boxes."

"Somehow, I don't think the window boxes are the expensive part," Bear said dryly. "And don't say I'll ask Rye for a bid—"

"You'd want to use him."

"Yes, but your brother isn't cheap."

"True, but he's good, and you can trust him. But if you want some other bids, I can do that."

"And offend Rye?"

She shrugged. "He knows it's business. Rye is the first one who would understand, especially now that you're friends. He'd never want you to feel awkward."

"Perhaps, but I'd rather have you work with him than some other random dude. Not all men are reliable and honest."

She laughed. "I'm tougher than I look, and if things ever got dicey, I have you and Rye on speed dial. Never mind Ansley's brother Lachlan on the Campbell ranch." Josie paused. "Speaking of Lachlan and the Campbell ranch, have you heard from Savannah at all?"

Bear shook his head. "No, but I gather she's been doing well. Rye did mention that Lachlan returns sometime next week so that might mean Savannah is on the move again."

"I hope not." Josie gave Bear a quick glance. "I like her tucked away in Paradise Valley. I find her far less threatening there."

"Why would you find her threatening? She can't hold a candle to you, Josie."

Josie couldn't answer without giving herself away.

"You're beautiful, Josie. The most beautiful woman I've ever met," he added, his voice deep.

Lifting her head she looked up into his eyes, seeing an intensity in his expression that stole her breath. She'd never seen that look in his eyes, but it was hot and fierce and also surprisingly possessive. "Men don't look at me."

"I'm looking at you."

"But it's different. You don't want me—"

"You can't say that."

Josie swallowed hard. "But I can. You're not interested in me romantically—"

"Again, not true. If I was the old Bear, I would have pursued you hard." A small muscle pulled in his square jaw. "You're the whole package. Perfect."

"But this new Bear isn't attracted to me?" she whispered, torn between mortification and curiosity. She needed to know what he was saying, needed to know if there was a chance for them.

Dusky color touched his cheekbones. "I'm very attracted to you."

"Seriously?"

"Yes, but I won't pursue you. I can't. I made that decision a long time ago."

"Why?"

He leaned back in his chair, brows lowering, light gray gaze narrowed. "It wouldn't be right."

He'd detached. Just like that. She could feel distance between them, the energy gone. "Why not?"

"You're very young."

"You're only ten years older."

"Eleven. Which is significantly older. And then I'm this—" He tapped the rim of his chair. "I'm not who I was, and I can't give you the life you deserve."

Her heart ached at that. "But you're wiser now than you were before."

"Wiser, and far more realistic. My life is full of challenges, and it's not a life for you. It's not a life I'd wish on anyone." His jaw eased and he gave his head a shake. "And that's not me feeling sorry for myself, I promise. There was a time I did feel sorry for myself, but I don't anymore. I've come to terms with what happened, and the fallout, and the past is the past. I'm trying my best to live in the now, and that means living with integrity and keeping it real."

She knew what he was saying, but she wasn't buying into his view. It certainly wasn't hers. That wasn't to say he was wrong—he was allowed to have his own opinions—but her opinion was that he was limiting himself, narrowing his options—and eliminating her as an option. It would be one thing if he wasn't attracted to her, but since he was, and as she was most definitely drawn to him, it didn't seem right that he could decide what was best for her.

"I like you," she said, voice husky. "A lot. I have from the first day we met."

"That's good, since we're roommates and friends."

Her chin lifted, her gaze locking with his. "We could be more."

"No, we can't. We're going to keep this platonic. We're going to put friendship and respect first—"

"Even if I'm dying to kiss you?"

He looked away, features tightening, cheekbones prominent. "You're not playing fair."

She leaned forward, one hand sliding across the table. "Don't you ever think about kissing me?"

Bear looked at her hard—nothing remotely tender in his eyes. No, he looked livid. Outraged. The seconds ticked by, each more painful than the last, before he turned and left the kitchen leaving her alone at the table with her sketchbook and their empty breakfast plates.

Josie blinked, and again, eyes burning, watering, throat aching. She sucked in her bottom lip and pressed it to her teeth. That had not gone well.

DON'T YOU EVER think about kissing me?

In his office, Bear covered his face with a hand, muscles tight, heart thudding. How could she do that to him? How could she test his resolve? It wasn't fair.

He thought about kissing her every single day, a dozen times a day or more.

He thought about pulling her onto his lap and wrapping her in his arms and holding her against him, savoring her softness and sweetness, pressing her breasts to his chest, letting his hands clasp her waist, and her beautifully rounded hips and butt. She was all curves, all warmth, all fire. Good God, he wanted her, desired her. But once he went there … once *they* went there … it was all over. He'd never be able to love her and let her go.

He'd never be able to look any other woman in the eyes or want to feel other lips against his. Perhaps there was another woman out there for him, perhaps there was someone who could settle for him, but he'd never ask it of Josie.

He'd never want less for her, only more.

Chapter Thirteen

DESPITE WAITING FOR hours, Rye didn't stop by the gallery, and between him failing to appear, and it being a excruciatingly slow day—just one person stopped in before leaving almost right away, muttering about the ridiculous prices on the painting—Josie couldn't wait until she could just go home.

It was awful when there was no one to distract her and she didn't know why the store was so empty and there seemed to be plenty of foot traffic, and all the parking spots on Main were full, but maybe it was just such a nice day that no one wanted to be inside looking at art.

The problem with being so alone was that she had far too much time on her hands to think, and today she couldn't stop thinking, her thoughts continuously circling back to Bear, and their conversation in the kitchen.

She remembered the flare of heat in his eyes, but also the anger.

She remembered how he abruptly wheeled out saying under his breath, no one was that good.

She remembered his words—he was attracted to her but wouldn't make a move.

Josie wanted to reach out to him and apologize for being so provocative earlier, but then stopped herself each time because she wasn't truly sorry. She was glad she'd said what she said. She was glad she pressed the point. She'd wanted to know how things stood, and now she did. Even if it wasn't the way she wanted things to be.

But what if she'd already pushed him too far? What if he was no longer comfortable having her around, in his house? What if he wanted her out?

Her heart fell at the thought, and stricken, she began cleaning in earnest, occupying her hands, if not her mind, by doing a deep clean, wiping down the baseboards, the impossible to reach corners of the floor, the edges of the gold frames, and then carefully dusting the rest.

Please don't be upset with me, she said under her breath as she sorted through the receipts and business cards in the drawer beneath the computer. *Don't be mad at me, Bear. I need you.*

Her eyes kept stinging and her hand shook ever so slightly as she sprayed a vinegar water mixture on the windows, polishing until they were streak free.

Josie wasn't built for drama, or unrequited love.

She didn't fall in love easily, and had only once been in love before, and that had been teenage love as a freshman in high school and he had been an upperclassman who didn't even know she existed. Now here she was, nine years later, in love again.

Emotionally worn out, Josie carried the cleaning supplies behind the curtain and rinsed off her hands in the small sink. A delicate bell rang, alerting her that the front door had opened. Josie emerged from behind the curtain to find Bear entering the gallery.

The tears she'd been fighting all day filled her eyes and she fought to hold them back. "Hey. What's going on?" she asked, smiling big, smiling hard, because she couldn't possibly cry and smile at the same time and if he saw her crying everything might just get weirder.

"How has the day been?"

"Good," she said, gesturing to the spotless but empty gallery. "I've been able to get caught up on cleaning and some organizing."

"But no buyers?"

"Not today."

"Want to get out for a bit? Could you close up for a half hour?" he asked.

Nothing sounded better but she wasn't sure. "What if that's when the next serious buyer arrives?"

"A serious buyer can wait a half hour. Put a sign in the window that says you'll be back at five thirty, and I promise to have you back by then."

Josie could use a breather and a reset. It had been a long day. Hastily, she scrawled CLOSED UNTIL 5:30 PM on a sheet of white paper, taped it on the inside of the front door, and locked up.

Outside, the temperature was warm enough that the late afternoon breeze felt particularly welcome. Just walking down Main Street felt good. She'd needed to stretch her legs and seeing Bear definitely lifted her spirits.

"Do we have a destination in mind or are we just walking?" she asked him, glancing at his profile.

"That new store across from the courthouse, the one you were so curious about this week, has opened. They just unveiled the sign today. Any idea what it is?"

She shook her head.

"Does a five-foot dancing ice cream cone help?"

"Ice cream shop?"

He nodded. "Tonight's their grand opening, the doors opened at five, and I thought we should be one of the ones first in line. You do like ice cream, don't you?"

"I love ice cream." There were few things she loved more than ice cream—cones, sundaes, milkshakes. "And from what Cormac's wife Whitney told me, there hasn't been an ice cream shop here since Scoop closed after Covid."

Bear had hoped they'd be one of the first in line at the new business, but as they approached the corner shop, a line stretched around the block, and down the street. "This might be longer than a half hour," Josie said as they joined the line.

"Maybe not," he answered. "Maybe they have a lot of servers working tonight. I imagine they would what with it being the grand opening."

Many of the people in line were parents with strollers and excited kids, but there was also an equal number of adults without kids waiting for their turn. Fortunately, the dancing ice cream cone—a dancing strawberry ice cream cone—was doing her best to entertain the kids with tap dancing, a little comedy, and silly songs. Parents smiled indulgently, but Josie studied the exterior of Lily's, charmed by the bold pink and white striped awning out front and the large old-fashioned, hand-painted sign reading Lily's Ice Cream in pink, white, and gold in the window.

Josie loved to know as much about everything as she could and so she pulled out her phone and did a search for Lily's Ice Cream Marietta, and discovered it was an original ice cream shop, founded by a fourth generation Montanan.

"Her great-great-grandfather arrived here from Germany via Chicago," Josie read to Bear, "bringing with him his love of all things Christmas and sweet. A new emigrant, he was just twenty-three when he was hired to work in the kitchen at the newly opened Blackstone Hotel in downtown Chicago. It was at Blackstone that he learned how to make ice cream, which had become wildly popular, and when he moved to Montana a decade later, he continued to make ice cream for his friends and family."

"Where are you finding all this information?" Bear asked.

Josie flashed her phone. "Her website."

"She has a website up already?"

"Yes, and so should you. Even if it just says *Coming*

Soon."

"What good would that do anyone?"

"They'd know something was in the works, and it might help answer questions that people might have. People are curious what you're doing with the Farrell Building."

"Some people know. I've had a visit from the chamber of commerce already wanting me to join."

"Did you?"

"Yes."

The line inched forward, and Josie could finally get a peek inside the window. The interior was pink and white with a classic soda fountain on one wall. "How yummy," she said. "I love it."

"It's very pink," Bear said.

Josie arched an eyebrow. "Does pink scare you?"

"Of course not."

"Is it a girl color?"

"*Josie.*"

She smiled mischievously. "Yes, dear?"

His eyes dropped to her mouth and lingered a moment, sending sparks of sensation through Josie's middle.

Bear cleared his throat. "Never mind. Dear."

The line did move quicker than Josie had expected and in less than ten minutes they were inside and discovering all the different flavors. Lily's featured seventeen original flavors, all made in house, with some rotating for the different seasons. Tonight, Lily's featured ice cream was a huckleberry cheesecake, with ribbons of thick huckleberry syrup, cream cheese and buttery graham cracker crust.

Josie tried the featured ice cream but then opted for a single scoop—which was still very large—of chocolate brownies and fudge ice cream—in one of Lily's homemade sugar cones. It was delicious.

They slowly made their way back to the gallery, Bear's ice cream in a cup between his knees, stopping periodically so Bear could take a bite.

They reached the gallery with five minutes to spare and stood outside to finish their ice cream. "This was a great idea," Josie said. "Thank you."

"I wanted to call you all day," he answered. "But I didn't know what to say. I never want to hurt your feelings and I know I did—"

"I'm to blame. I started it, and I shouldn't have been so provocative. I put you in a weird position. I'm sorry."

He used his paper napkin to reach up and swipe the corner of her mouth which turned out to have some extra ice cream. "You can't take this personally," he said quietly. "You're an amazing woman. I respect you and admire you—"

"I'd rather you think I'm hot and impossible to resist."

Bear grinned. "You are hot, and very hard to resist, but I do respect you, and I want the best for you." His smile faded. "You mean a lot to me. You've made everything better. I don't want to lose you, or your friendship."

Josie maintained her smile even as she silently counted to

five. "You won't," she said when she was certain she could keep her voice steady. "Friends for life."

Bear waited until she'd unlocked the gallery door and taken down the paper sign to leave. Josie stood at one of the tall sparkling windows and watched him go, telling herself that being friends with him was better than nothing. But being friends with him also felt terrible sometimes. Kind of like now, when all she wanted was a hug, and maybe a kiss.

MUCH OF THE next week was spent at the Farrell Building. Framing was happening inside, bathroom and office walls going up, while holes were being cut in the ceiling for the five skylights that were supposed to arrive any day now.

Josie had spent a great deal of time researching flooring options for the huge space. Ceramic tiles were good for heavy electric chairs, but they were hard and bruising if one fell on them, and Bear's clientele would probably take some falls. Nonslip vinyl was recommended for bathrooms, and Josie ordered samples of that, along with samples of rubber flooring for the facility itself.

She had the various materials laid out for Bear to look at and was just waiting for him to get off the phone. He finally hung up, but he wasn't happy as he joined her in an area without construction.

"Bad news?" she asked, reading his expression.

"Skylights were supposed to be here tomorrow, but they're missing."

"Missing where? Missing how?"

He shrugged, his powerful shoulders rolling. "No one seems to know but everyone says they're working on it, so we'll see." He turned his attention to the materials spread out on the floor. "What is that one?" he asked, pointing to a beige and white diamond pattern.

"It's a nonslip vinyl."

"I don't like it. It looks like something in a hospital."

"Probably because it's good for wheelchairs." She leaned over and pushed aside the beige and white pattern, revealing a cobalt blue vinyl. "You can do something really bold in here. You don't have to do hospital beige."

"I don't think an all-blue floor would be appealing. And I'm not sure I'd like it with red brick." He looked to see what else she had spread on the ground. "That looks like something in my old gym."

"It's rubber flooring, which is the preferred flooring in gyms." She picked up a big square and handed it to him. "The material absorbs well, which is great for preventing falls, and you could do different color blocks, which would visually expand the space and make it more stylish, depending on the color patterns you choose."

"I sense an objection."

"Installation is time consuming, so your labor is expensive. It will smell rubbery in here for the first couple of months after installation."

"Or years," Bear muttered.

She nodded. "But on the plus side, rubber is good for ramps, and spaces that get wet. Come wintertime with rain and snow, your rubber floor will have better traction than other flooring materials."

"Everyone that comes through those doors will be in a wheelchair, and they'll be rolling through everything that's on the ground—snow, mud, slush, gravel, dirt."

"Which is why the rubber flooring would be a good choice, and you have quite a few solid colors to pick from." She reached for a brochure and opened it, showing him the fifteen options. "I'd probably do a mix of colors, charcoal, capri blue, maybe pearl and one other color. Your entrance and path through the facility could be one color, and then you could highlight work out areas with two other colors. With the height of the ceiling, and the red brick, and sky lights having some visual interest on the floor—in my mind—would look best and keep the facility from looking institutional."

Bear shuddered. "God only knows I've had enough of that."

"And everyone else that comes here to work out." Josie folded the brochure. "Have you thought about a catchy name for your business? I struggle to explain what you're doing when I talk to people. Facility sounds like you sort mail and gym makes me think of guys and girls flexing in front of a mirror and taking selfies in between sets."

"I know. I'm leaning toward spinal cord injured people might recognize—Training Facility for SC Injuries, or Exo Gym for SC Injuries. I don't like any of them but I'm sure we'll figure it out."

Sixty minutes later, they were done meeting with Rye and his various contractors. Bear and Josie left the Farrell Building, stepping out into the late afternoon light and sighing at the quiet.

"That was noisy in there," she said.

"Masonry saws are notoriously loud, but that was a lot. Once they're done opening up the storage room to the rest of the building, it should get quieter."

"Now you just need your skylights."

"Oh—I got a text on that. Hang on." Bear retrieved his phone, scrolled through messages. "Here it is. The skylights have been found. They're in Marietta." He looked up at her, amused. "Marietta, South Dakota."

"You're kidding me!"

"At least they've been found and are being shipped here tomorrow. We should have them by the end of the week."

"Agreed."

They crossed the street heading toward Main reaching Bear's truck first. "I have a Zoom call in a half hour. What are you going to do now? Errands, or head back to the house?"

"I'm going to stop by the gallery—Ansley has a check for

me—and then I can pick up dinner. How does French dip sound for tonight?"

"Wonderful."

"Since you have that Zoom, I'll probably hang out with Ansley for a bit before ordering. How long do you think you'll be on the call?"

"I should be done by six."

"Perfect. I'll be home with dinner then."

At the gallery, Josie couldn't believe the check Ansley handed to her. It was a significant amount of money.

"This is crazy," Josie said, looking at the check and then her sister-in-law. "This is way too much money."

"Not at all. You've earned it. I don't know how you do it, but you make the pictures fly off the wall."

"I do nothing. I just point to your work and your talent is obvious. Your work sells itself."

"You're very sweet."

"I'm very proud of you." Josie suddenly remembered the Sheenan project at Flathead Lake. "Has Whitney Sheenan been in contact with you about the painting they want for their lake cottage?"

"She has, and she's offered their cottage to Rye and me for a couple of weeks in September so that I can paint and be inspired."

"That's a pretty nice offer."

"I'm looking forward to it. Rye and I haven't been away since our honeymoon. We could both use a little downtime together."

"What about Mick? Do you want us to keep him while you're gone?"

"Oh no. Mick would come with us. I couldn't leave him behind. He's been through so much and he's just beginning to feel secure again."

Josie checked her smile. "Rye told Bear that Mick has become very attached to you."

"Mick still loves jumping in the truck and going on job sites with Rye, but once he's home, he sticks close to my side. I've become quite attached to him."

Josie glanced at her wall clock and saw that is was almost five forty-five. "I'm going to pick up dinner at the diner. Do you want me to get anything for you and Rye?"

"I made enchiladas this morning before work. Rye has already put them in the oven."

Josie kissed Ansley's cheek and left the gallery. It had clouded over earlier in the day and the sky was dark and stormy. It rarely rained in summer, but the clouds looked black enough that Josie wouldn't be surprised if they didn't get a few drops.

For fifteen minutes, she sat inside the diner waiting for her order to be prepared, while scrolling on her phone and keeping an eye on the weather outside. The wind was blowing and with the heavy clouds hanging low in the sky it looked far later than it was.

As soon as the waitress brought Josie her order, she

stepped outside, the wind extra gusty, tangling her hair and blowing it across her face.

She peeled back the tendril clinging to her eye lashes and dashed across the street to her car when another gust of wind nearly ripped the plastic bag out of her hands. She dug through her oversized tote for her car keys but couldn't find her keys. She hadn't left them at the gallery, had she?

Josie stepped back to the curb, and bent over to set the dinner bag down, but somehow tripped on the curb edge and went down, hard, sending her purse and dinner flying. She heard the containers pop open and could just imagine the au jus spilling everywhere.

"Dang it, girl, be careful," a gravel-voiced man boomed, extending a hand and hauling her none to gently to her feet.

Straightening, Josie stiffened, thinking the man's face and voice were strangely familiar. It took her a split second to place him. Eureka, her hometown. Darren Clark, the car salesman who'd served two terms on the city council. Darren Clark, the man who'd shut her down when she'd gone to city hall asking for donations for the humane society.

"Hello, Mr. Clark," she said faintly, stunned to see him here in Marietta of all places.

He frowned at her, not yet recognizing her. "Do I know you?"

"We're both from Eureka. I met you years ago when I was twelve." Josie crouched back down to scoop up the dripping sandwich and set it more securely in its carboard box. The au jus was gone, having puddled either into the bread, or onto the pavement.

"Did you win some spelling bee or something?" he asked, watching her drop the small cup and lid into the plastic bag, on top of the ruined sandwich.

"No. I asked if you could contribute to a fundraiser, and you said no." She looked up at him, forcing a smile. "But it was a long time ago. I can't expect you to remember every little girl that comes asking for help."

"Wait a minute. I do know you. You're John's girl."

She rose and wiped her damp hand on the back of her jeans. "You do remember."

"Looks like you've ruined your dinner. What was it?" he asked, glancing down into her soggy bag. "French dip?"

"Main Street Diner's Monday night special."

"Let me go buy you another sandwich."

"I'll make these work. Throw them under the broiler. It'll be fine."

"Fresh ones would taste better. Nobody likes a soggy bun."

"I don't want to waste the money. But if you'd like to make a donation, Marietta has several pet rescues that would welcome the support."

Darren Clark barked a laugh. "Still a bleeding heart?"

"I still care about the less fortunate. One of my best qualities, I've been told."

"You look a lot like your mother. How is she?"

"Good."

"Still with your father?"

"Of course."

"No of course about it. She was one of the saddest ladies I ever met. Your dad didn't do right by her. She deserved better."

Her stomach knotted, and she flexed a hand at her side. "And you told her that, right?"

"She knew how I felt, and she knew I would have taken care of her."

Josie felt like a fish out of water, her mouth opening and closing but no sound came out. She was shocked, shocked silent.

Darren looked her up and down, sizing her up. "She was soft, and it got her hurt. You can't go through life soft, girl. To get ahead in this world, you have to put yourself first." He tipped the brim of his hat in her direction and started off down the sidewalk.

Josie watched him a moment, insides churning, emotions in turmoil. She took several steps after him. "What are you doing here in Marietta, Mr. Clark?"

He turned to look at her. "What?"

"Are you on vacation, or is this home now?"

"I've bought a place here."

"I live here, too, now, as does my brother Rye—"

"What about your dad and that crippled brother of yours?"

"My dad, my brother, and my *mom* are outside Bozeman. I hope they'll never run into you."

"I'm not the villain here, girl, no need to be mad at me. Your dad was the one who let the family down. Your dad was the one who couldn't take care of all of you."

"Who are you to judge him?"

"I'm simply a realist, girl."

"And a bully."

He shrugged impatiently. "It's about survival. Being responsible. But not everyone wants what you want, and they shouldn't have to pay for changes that don't help them."

"Like what?"

"Schools for crippled kids, camps and sports for special kids. Ramps and lifts for older buildings. Why is it my problem that your brother couldn't get in to some of Eureka's buildings? Why should I have to pay more taxes because he has problems?"

"Because we're supposed to take care of each other. We're supposed to love our neighbor—"

"Oh, I love my neighbor, as long as they don't bother me, I don't bother them."

Josie had had enough. She threw her shoulders back and held her head high. "Have a good evening, Mr. Clark, and hopefully I won't see you again anytime soon."

He opened his mouth to say something before thinking better of it. Muttering beneath his breath, he cut across the street, passing between cars, forcing one driver to slam on the brakes. The driver then laid on his horn, hard.

Darren lifted a hand and gave the driver the finger.

Josie watched and shook her head. The world was full of monsters and beasts but at least at home she had her Bear.

BEAR COULD TELL something was upsetting Josie the moment she entered the house. She said it was because she'd dropped their dinner and had ruined the sandwiches, but he knew it was more than that. She wasn't annoyed or frustrated as much as completely flattened.

"What's wrong?" he asked, joining her in the kitchen where she was just standing at the counter, staring at nothing.

She shook her head. "Just tired, I think."

"This isn't tired. This is something else. I don't know if you're sad, or mad, but something happened."

Still facing the cabinets, she reached up to swipe beneath one eye and then the next. "Some people are just a-holes. It's like they love to be horrible and love to be unkind. Why?"

"Because it makes them feel powerful and better about themselves." He took her hand and tugged her around so that she would face him.

She fought to stop the tears, but they kept falling anyway. He wanted to know what happened, but at the same time, he just wanted to comfort her. Bear pulled her down onto his lap and wrapped his arms around her. She pressed her face to his chest and cried. He'd never heard her cry like this. She sounded absolutely broken.

He cupped the back of her head, his palm smoothing her hair, even as he kissed her temple, murmuring that everything was okay, that he had her, that nothing could happen now.

He felt her take a deep shuddering breath, and then she lifted her head, her eyes like wet pansies. So beautiful.

"Can you tell me what happened?" he asked quietly, using his thumbs to wipe away the tears.

"I bumped into a horrible man. I knew him from Eureka, and he remembered my dad and mom. And Jasper." She swallowed hard. "He was so demeaning toward my brother. The things he said—" She broke off, her brow darkening, as if remembering what he'd said or perhaps there was something else on her mind. "What is wrong with people?

"What did he say?" Bear persisted.

She shook her head. "I just hope I never see him again."

"Well, if you do, point him out and I'll knock his head off his block for you."

Josie laughed and smiled at him, her smile lighting her eyes, making her the Josie he knew and adored.

"I would love that," she confided. "I don't usually condone violence but in this case, it's completely justified."

Then Bear did what he had vowed he'd never do—his mouth covered hers and he kissed her, and it wasn't just a little kiss. No, once his mouth claimed hers, there was no letting her go, no way to not taste her and love her.

She was the most extraordinary woman.

He clasped her face, angling her head to better touch, lick, nip. She was so responsive, too, shivering and whimpering, pressing herself against him, her arms around his shoulders, her bottom in his hands and of course he caressed her, hearing her sigh, and pant as he slipped his hand between her thighs. He stroked her through her jeans and yet she jerked at the touch. He stroked her again, drawing circles and, crying out, she pulled back to stare into his eyes, her expression dazed and desperate all at the same time.

"Can't do this here," she whispered.

"Can't do this anywhere," he rasped, slowly coming to his senses. Blood pounded in his veins. Desire burned through him. "This shouldn't have happened. I shouldn't have done that."

She was still fighting to catch her breath. "Yes, you should have. You're a really good kisser."

"I don't think it's relevant."

"Of course it's relevant. And I didn't want to stop. I just hoped we could go to your room where we could be more comfortable."

"That's a big fat no. That will not happen. Kissing you was a mistake and mistakes do not need to be repeated because then it's just plain stupidity."

"Cowboy, it's not as if we were doing the nasty. It was a

kiss. I think you should relax."

"Maybe you should get off my lap."

"Nope." She leaned in, her arms wrapped around his neck. "I like it here. It's really nice."

"You're impossible."

"Thank you." She kissed the side of his neck, breathing in the hint of his aftershave. "You smell delicious, too."

"Josie."

"Yes, Bear?" she said, kissing a spot beneath his ear.

"You're not fair."

"I'm tired of fair. Because it's not actually fair." She brushed her lips across his. "I dig you. Everything about you. But I think you know that."

He dragged his fingers through her hair, scraping the long length back from her face, knotting the strands around his fist and gently but firmly tugging her head back. "I'm trying to do the right thing. I'm trying my best to protect you." He gave another little tug on her hair, and she shuddered, her hips dancing on his lap.

"I don't need protection. Not from you." Her voice dropped. She raked her nails down his cheek. "And for your information, kissing me was not a disaster. Kissing me made us both feel better."

"You think so?"

"I know so." She drew a quick, tremulous breath. "And it's something I've needed for weeks."

He cupped her face and stared into her eyes. "You're killing me, Josie."

"I think resisting me is killing you. Maybe stop doing that and just kiss me the way you to want. The way I want you to."

He did.

JOSIE SLEPT THAT night in his room, in his bed. There were no more kisses, and everything was as circumspect as could be, except for the fact that Bear slept with his arm around her, and she didn't think she'd ever felt anything as wonderful as being pressed up against his big chest, his hand laced through hers.

She knew he'd have to move in the night, and adjust the pillow between his knees, but it was the perfect way to fall asleep. It was peaceful and healing, and it answered the ache within her for more closeness. She loved him. She wanted a life with him. She wanted to be there at his side every day, for the good days and the bad.

But she knew he wasn't ready to hear that. He'd been through a lot with Savannah, and he still worried about burdening those around him, and so she kept her love and commitment to herself. With time, he'd see how it was with them. With time, he'd realize how good they were together. Rome wasn't built in a day. Winning Bear's heart would take time, too.

It was enough for now to just savor his warmth, his arm wrapped around her, his body to her back, the steady rise and fall of his chest calming, reassuring.

Life could be hard, but it was also beautiful.

Her Bear was beautiful, too.

Chapter Fourteen

THE NEXT TWO weeks passed in a blur of work and play. Bear agreed that a little kissing and cuddling was fine, but he drew the line at getting naked and intimate.

Josie suspected it was scary for him—his body had changed, making love would be different. She didn't have a tremendous amount of experience so she wasn't sure how it would all work, but she loved him so much that she wasn't afraid, and she was happy to give him, and them, time.

The month of August was almost over, and Labor Day was approaching. Everyone was making plans to do something, but Josie had no desire to go anywhere and do anything but be with Bear.

"Do you think we should invite my parents and Jasper over for Labor Day weekend? We could grill—well, you could grill—and I could handle the rest. I know Jasper is dying to meet you."

"Are you sure that's a good idea?" he asked.

"Why wouldn't it be?"

He shrugged. "Might be a little awkward for everyone."

"You mean three wheelchairs at dinner? We'll call it the wheelchair friendship club."

Bear groaned and shook his head. "That's horrible."

"It's kind of funny."

"It's not." But he couldn't help smiling a little.

Josie called her parents that evening to see if they'd like to come for dinner over the weekend. "I'd love for you to see Bear's house and everything we did to make it work for him."

"I don't know," her mom answered. "Jasper's been tired lately, and I'm not sure driving all that way for dinner is a good idea. Maybe you could just come home and spend the weekend with us?"

"Don't you want to meet Bear?"

"Honey, we'll meet him sometime when the timing is better. But give him our best, okay?"

Josie hung up disappointed but decided not to say anything to Bear that evening. Maybe she could give it a few days and try talking to her dad. Or maybe it was just too early, and her mom was right, she needed to hold off and wait for another time.

WHAT JOSIE DIDN'T know was that Bear had received a call from Jennifer Calhoun, Josie's mother, asking him to meet her for coffee. She thought it was time they met and hoped he wouldn't mind not saying anything to Josie about their get together.

Bear thought it was a peculiar request, but he knew Josie was sensitive about her family and didn't want to upset her. So, he drove to the coffee shop in Livingston where Jennifer had suggested they meet as it was a good halfway point for both of them.

He spotted Jennifer right away. She looked like an older version of Josie, only a Josie that hadn't aged as well as she could have.

"Mrs. Calhoun," he said, approaching.

She nodded and smiled, but the smile didn't reach her eyes. "Thank you so much for meeting with me," she said, clearly nervous.

"I'm happy to meet you. You must know I'm a fan of both your son and daughter."

"Thank you. I'm a fan, too. I have great kids. I'm really lucky."

"Let's get you inside. It's a hot one today," he said, leaning forward to open the door and holding it open until she was safely inside. He followed, the door bumping the back tire of his chair as it closed behind him.

They ordered drinks at the counter and then found a table in the back corner, away from the bright sunlight glaring against the glass. At the small table, Bear pulled out a chair, pushing it to the table next to theirs to create room for him.

Jennifer looked around. "I've never been here before."

"I haven't, either. How did you learn about it?"

"Rye once mentioned it, said it was a good place to meet

up, in case I ever wanted to get out for a bit."

"You should meet him."

"Hard to get away."

The barista arrived at their table with their drinks. "Iced coffee with milk," she said, handing Jennifer her order. "And a black coffee for you," she said, placing Bear's cup on the table.

Bear sipped his coffee and waited for Jennifer to speak. She'd requested the meeting, and he was curious as to what she wanted to say.

"I don't know how much you know about my family," she said after a moment, nudging her glass. "I was born and raised in Alberta, Canada. I met John—the kids' dad—in Calgary. I was young, early twenties, and within six months of meeting, John and I were married. It was a whirlwind courtship, but the biggest reason we married so quickly was that I was pregnant with Rye."

Bear simply listened, having no desire to speak.

"We loved each other," Jennifer continued, "so it wasn't a bad thing to marry quickly, but marriage is hard. There is no road map with it, and everyone handles difficulties differently." She paused, her fine dark eyebrows drawing together. "John and I have had good years and bad years. That's what marriage is. You don't get the good without the bad. I know that. And we are blessed by our children. I consider myself very fortunate with that in that regard."

"You are a devoted mom."

"Sometimes they were all that kept me going." She hesitated, expression troubled. "In general, I don't think I'm a pushy mom, or an overly protective mom, but when it comes to Josie I worry."

Rye just waited. Now that he was here, he had all the time in the world.

Jennifer smiled nervously, her hands clenching together on the edge of the table. "All of my kids are special, and they all have unique attributes, but Josie is different. She's such a love. She has been my cuddle bug since she was just a little girl. But not just with me, with the entire family. She was the first to wake up and give hugs. She was the one who'd sneak into your room at night and give you one last kiss. She'd do everything in her power to make people happy, to make us, her family, happy. When John would be drinking and impossible, Josie would still go to him and try to talk sense into him, trying to divert his attention from whatever was making him angry."

Bear's chest ached, and he hadn't realized he'd been holding his breath until he had to exhale. "Did your husband take it out on you?"

"He was never rough physically. It was his moods more than anything. He got in a very dark place and there wasn't much I could do until he sobered up." She looked away, cheeks pink, her mouth quivering slightly. "Josie sometimes forgets to protect herself. John never hit her—or any of us—but he certainly wasn't always kind."

Bear didn't think he'd ever like Josie's dad now.

"You know, Josie only moved out a year ago. Until then, she's always been with us."

And still Bear bit his tongue. What was the point of this? Where was she going?

"It's good for Josie to be out of our house and finding herself. Every young person needs that time to discover who they really are, which is why I don't want Josie to jump into anything too fast. I don't want her to lead with her heart, but that's what she does. It's what I used to do. I was a lot like Josie, and I thought love was magic, love would conquer everything. But it doesn't work that way. A successful relationship requires more than love and I just want her to have time. I want her to gain more experience. I want her to have some adventures and to focus on herself. I want her to not be me, and rush into forever, before you really know what you're doing."

"You're afraid that I'm rushing Josie into a commitment."

Jennifer shook her head. "No. My fear is that Josie is rushing herself into a commitment." She looked at Bear, brow creased, her lavender blue eyes revealing her anxiety. "I hate putting you in this position, but I didn't know what else to do, and I don't want her to do what I did. Because when you're young, you just don't know how long life can be, and how much crap it can throw at you." She paused and waited, as if needing confirmation.

He nodded, once. It was that or nothing. He couldn't bring himself to speak, not then.

"Bear, she clearly cares for you a great deal, and I can see why she does. You're handsome and strong and inspiring, and she only sees the beautiful things, she doesn't realize what it could be like..."

Her voice faded. She didn't finish the thought. But Bear understood what she wanted to say but wouldn't let herself.

"You are afraid that with me being injured, it will be hard on her," Bear said. "You're afraid she won't have the life you want for her."

Jennifer clenched the table's edge. "You must see this isn't about you. This is about me, and my experiences, and how I struggled over the years with having been dealt a challenging hand."

"I'm not judging you."

"It was so difficult when Jasper was born, so difficult to get him stable, so difficult to keep him alive. It felt like we spent half of our life at the hospital, praying that our sweet boy would survive the night. But at least I had John at my side. But then when John fell and broke his back, I lost him ... we were no longer equals, I became his caregiver, too."

"I can't imagine."

"We'd all depended on him, but after he was hurt, he withdrew, struggling with depression and anger. I thought the depression would be temporary, but they became part of him. His personality changed. I didn't blame him then, because how do you reconcile your world changing in the blink of an eye? John was a proud man and tough. Athletic. He wanted to be the John who wasn't hurt. He wanted to be the man he'd been before his fall."

"I can relate."

Tears filled her eyes and she struggled to hold his gaze. "I'm sure you can." Her voice dropped to a mere whisper. "Which is why this is so hard for me."

Bear reached across the table and took her hand. "It's okay," he said, feeling how she trembled. "Everything is fine. Don't be afraid."

"I don't want to hurt you."

"You can't," he said gently, kindly. "You won't."

Jennifer blinked and a tear fell. Impatiently, she brushed it away reminding him all over again of Josie. "Our move to Park County last year changed things for all of us. John is doing better. Jasper is healthier and happier and wanting to start college. The girls are both finishing their education. Rye is married to wonderful Ansley. Things are good. They should be good. But one thing hasn't changed."

Bear's chest felt bruised. Each breath hurt. "You're still the caregiver," he said. "And you will always be the caregiver."

She nodded. "I'm not complaining, but it is the reality I live with. There have been times where I wanted to run away, but of course I didn't. I couldn't. Jasper…" She swallowed hard and put a hand across her eyes, struggling to put her intense feelings into words. "But you see, you see why I'm protective of Josie. You see why I want you—I *need* you—to be careful with her." Another tear fell. "And not encourage her. She is lovely, and she has the heart of an angel. She never thinks of herself, so her family—those of us who love her—have to do that for her. We have to remind her that she's important, and her dreams are important, and those dreams should be protected. Even if she doesn't yet know what those dreams are."

THEY LEFT THE Livingston coffee shop without either of them touching their drinks. Bear walked Jennifer to her car and waited for her to drive away before heading to his truck.

Once inside his truck, he sat motionless for a long time. Jennifer had said so much. It had been a torrent of words, of fear, of pain. It was a lot to take in, almost too much for Bear to process.

A dark weariness swept over him as he drove the ten miles back to Marietta. He was exhausted in a way he hadn't been since first moving from the hospital to the rehab facility and he had to learn how to do everything again, so daunting when just learning how to transfer to a wheelchair from a hospital bed had overwhelmed him. It wasn't just learning how to navigate the transfer, it was the specific muscles that needed strength, the confidence that he could do it, the realization that his legs would never be able to support him again. There would be no steps, no running, no speed—not unless his upper body could do it for him.

He knew he was lucky to be a para not a quad. He was lucky that eventually he'd have independence again. He was lucky that he had a woman who loved him, a woman who'd support him.

Until Savannah couldn't be that woman, unable to handle the changes, unable to see a future for them now.

She ended the engagement and didn't disappear from his life completely, just slowly weaning herself off, finding comfort with others since he couldn't comfort her the way she needed.

He was the one who told her she didn't need to come see him anymore when it was clear to them both that she didn't like visiting him, that she spaced the visits out, from every day to every other day, and then every three days, and then just once a week.

She said she had work. She was playing at the Bluebird. She was writing music. She had to go into the studio and cut a new track. She had an excuse for everything. And she expected him to understand. She expected him to be okay with her disappearing on him and he was, he supposed, provided it just stopped.

No more uncomfortable visits. No more pecks on his cheek. No more stilted conversation about his rehabilitation.

She didn't like the rehab facility filled with men in hospital beds with wheelchairs at the sides.

And then there was the time someone asked for Savannah's autograph as she left. He was a male nurse and he recognized Savannah, having seen her at different venues, and he'd bought one of her CDs after a show.

Savannah, who had barely smiled at Bear that visit, now glowed with gratitude, and took the time to visit with her smitten fan. It was then Bear knew they were done. He wasn't angry as much as resigned. They'd been through so much together, but the stress had driven them apart instead of bringing them closer.

Bear parked in front of his house, his boxy, plain little house with the beautiful interior, a space Josie had labored over to get it just right for him.

He swallowed, his eyes hot and gritty. He felt like hell. His world had shattered again. His chest seized, everything tight and hard.

It was over. He and Josie were done.

Chapter Fifteen

BEAR HAD RETURNED from his trip to Clyde Park unusually quiet and withdrawn. Josie couldn't get two words out of him. He set his keys in the bowl on the narrow hall table, simply disappeared into his room and stayed there, claiming he had a headache and just needed some time in the dark, alone.

Josie couldn't leave him alone, though, not when she was worried. She rapped lightly on his closed door. "Bear, I have some ibuprofen and water. It'll help you feel better."

"I don't want anything." His voice was a growl from behind the closed door. "I just need some time."

She heard something different in his voice, something dark, something sharp, and it made her afraid. What had happened while he was gone?

She finally forced herself to leave his room, but it felt awful leaving him when he was in pain. He'd been fine earlier. He'd left the house in a good mood. He'd kissed her before he left, and he'd lightly touched her cheek as he smiled into her eyes and called her his sweet girl.

It was hours before Bear emerged from his room. Josie had made herself a turkey sandwich and nibbled on half even though it tasted like cardboard. She hated feeling anxious, but she was worried for Bear, worried he'd hurt himself, worried that something was broken or causing him terrible pain.

She was sitting on one end of the leather sectional in the living room when he rolled into the room.

"We have to talk," he said.

His tone sent an arrow of ice straight through her. "Okay."

He positioned himself across the room from her. He didn't transfer to his recliner, but sat forward, his big forearms resting on his knees.

He didn't speak for a long minute and then he lifted his head and looked at her, no warmth or emotion in his eyes. "This isn't working. I've known it for the past few weeks, and I was a coward and didn't say anything, but I can't hide from the truth anymore. We can't continue like this."

It was even worse than she thought.

Josie gripped her hands in her lap, fighting for her composure. "I don't believe you."

"You should." His tone was harsh, blunt, brutal, and he didn't look away, he just stared into her as if she was nothing at all.

"What happened, Bear? What did I do wrong?"

Bear growled deep in his throat. "There's nothing wrong with you. This isn't because there's something wrong with *you*. It's because there's something wrong with me."

"Because you can't walk?"

"Because there's a million things I can't do—"

"Not true. There are more things you can do than not do. You're a remarkable human being, and you have everything I want in a person, a partner. You are everything I care about. You are smart, tough, compassionate, hard-working, honest, loyal, and gorgeous. I guess I'm allowed to be a little bit shallow. Your legs may not be working, Bear, but your face is."

"Let's cut to the chase. I can't have sex. I can't give you kids. I will have a lifetime of health complications, and I don't want to put you through that."

"If we wanted kids we could adopt. There's lots of ways to be intimate without intercourse. And everyone has issues at different points in their life. Everyone has health problems."

"It's one thing to develop them later in a relationship. It's another to start off a relationship with everything stacked against you."

"I just don't see it that way."

"I appreciate your generous spirit, but when it comes to a relationship, both opinions matter, and my feelings on this are really strong. It's not a little hang up. It's a serious issue, and I'm not going to change my mind."

She rose to go to him, but he rolled away. "Don't touch me," he gritted.

She flinched as if slapped but she held her ground, determined to fight. "We can work though this, Bear. If you give us a chance."

"That's just it. I'm not going to give us a chance. I can't do it. I won't do it."

"But Bear, I love you—"

"You don't." His voice was hard, ruthless.

"Why are you doing this? What's happened? Something happened, because this morning everything was good. Last night, everything was great."

He shrugged. "I was faking it."

"You weren't. I know you."

"But that's just it. You don't know me. You don't know me at all."

She tossed her head back, jaw firm, tears shimmering in her eyes. "You're an ass."

"Exactly. That *is* me, the real me. Ask Savannah. She'll tell you. I am selfish. I am hard. I am driven and self-absorbed and everything that is not good for you. I am not good for you, Josie, and I'm going to be honest, you are not good for me."

"*Why?*"

"You're too soft, too sweet, too innocent, too hopeful. Sweetheart, you are beautiful, and I have a thing for your face. I have a thing for your eyes and that mouth and everything about you. I'm turned on by your sweet little package and I could get lost in your body, but once I've had enough, once I've had my fill—" He broke off, shook his head. "I'll still be Bear Anderson, and Bear Anderson only cares about Bear Anderson. I'm not father material. I'm not boyfriend material. I'm not husband material. I was a good lover—and that's the one thing I can't do anymore. So sorry, sweets, I have nothing for you."

"You're just afraid," she choked.

He shrugged. "Maybe, or maybe I've finally grown a conscience—"

"You've had a conscience this entire time. You went out of your way to apologize to me after our bumpy first meeting!"

"Then maybe I've just wised up and realized that as fun as it was playing house with you, it's not fun anymore. I like you. I enjoy your company. But I don't love you. I won't ever love you, and it's better for us to make a clean break of it now, before things progress any further."

"You want me to move out?"

"I think you should."

Her lips parted and then closed. She glanced away and blinked, holding back the tears. "I'll need a few days. Rye and Ansley are going to a wedding in Missoula this weekend but once Rye's home…"

"Not a problem. I'm traveling myself. I leave for Austin in the morning."

She looked at him puzzled. "Are you meeting Dillon Sheenan?"

"And some of his friends. It's a week trip, I'll be back by

the weekend."

She nodded once.

"I'm sorry about how things worked out," he said, his tone softening for the first time since they began talking, "but it really is for the best."

"I'll go stay at Rye's tonight and pack up the small things tomorrow once you're gone. By the time you're back, the house will be all yours."

JOSIE HADN'T CRIED on the drive to Rye's, and she didn't cry as she let herself into the dark house.

"I'm house-sitting for them," Savannah said. "And taking care of Mick." She nodded at the dog who had checked out Josie and then went to his dog bed in the corner and lay down. "What are you doing here?"

The last thing Josie wanted to do was talk to Savannah, but seeing as Savannah was supposed to be here and Josie wasn't, Josie had to say something. "I needed a place to stay tonight. Do you mind if I crash here for the night?"

"Did you and Bear have a fight?" Savannah asked, putting a kettle on the stove.

Josie wasn't even sure how to answer that. "I don't know what happened," she said, unsteadily, trying to keep all the emotion in check. "But the bottom line is that he asked me to move out, and tomorrow I'll do that. Or at least everything I can get without Rye's help."

Savannah appeared dumbfounded. "What happened?"

"I don't know. He … flipped a switch. Everything was fine and then it wasn't." The tears Josie had been holding back were back, but she didn't want to cry, not in front of Savannah.

"There has to be more." Savannah gestured to a barstool at the counter. "Sit down, I'll make us some tea."

Josie was grateful to sit. She was shaking, her legs weak, her insides churning. She felt wrecked and stunned. She still couldn't make sense of what had happened.

"Did you have a fight?" Savannah asked, retrieving a box of herbal tea from the cupboard.

"No. We had coffee together yesterday, chatted about our days. He had some meetings and things. I was going to work on my notes and sketches for my design project for school, and when he returned, he was … different. Very quiet and remote. He went straight to his room and stayed there for hours. When he came out, he said we had to talk, and it was over."

"So, you are involved. Not just friends." But Savannah didn't say it unkindly. Her tone was matter of fact.

Josie nodded. "It hasn't been long. Just a couple of weeks."

"And that was going well?" Savannah asked, dropping a teabag in each mug.

"I thought it was. We get along really well. Bear didn't

want it to become more than friends. I was the one who did. I wouldn't say I seduced him, but I wanted more with him. I'm crazy attracted to him."

"And he to you, I imagine."

Josie nodded. "I thought we were doing well. I thought we'd become a pretty solid us." She glanced at Savannah and then away. "But this evening when Bear finally came out of his room tonight, he was a different person. He said the past couple of weeks were a mistake. And that I needed to leave." Her voice broke, and Josie wiped at her eyes, determined to keep it together. "I'm sorry. I'm sorry to dump on you like this."

"It's fine. If anyone knows Bear, it's me." The kettle began to whistle, and Savannah lifted it off the burner. "But this doesn't sound like him. Bear is complex, but he's steady. Solid. Bear doesn't flip out for no reason. I'm shocked, to be honest. I've been jealous of you two."

"You have?"

"Mmmm. Bear is so sweet with you. He's a different person with you. Which makes me think there's something else behind this. Something else that set him off. Bear is tough, but he's fair, and this doesn't sound fair."

"I've been racking my brain, trying to figure out what I might have done, but I can't think of anything. Last night was good, and our coffee this morning was good. I'd hoped my family would come over this weekend for a barbecue, but my brother has been tired, and my mom didn't think it would be good to drag him over to Marietta."

"Why didn't she have you and Bear come see them at their house?"

"Bad timing, she said." Josie bit her lip. She felt so raw and so confused. Nothing made sense. She was grateful to have someone to talk to, even if it was Bear's ex. "Is that how your relationship ended? Kind of out of the blue?"

"No. Not the way you think." Savannah filled their cups with hot water and carried them over to the counter, pushing one in front of Josie before sitting down on a stool.

Savannah's long fair hair was in a loose braid, and she had no makeup on and still looked stunning. Josie didn't think it was fair. Savannah was beautiful and talented and here in Marietta … waiting for Bear to be available?

"Are you hoping to get back together with Bear?" Josie asked, voice quavering. "I won't be mad. I just need to know."

"Bear and I will never get back together." Savannah's voice was firm, and she gave Josie a rueful smile. "Bear might love me, but he doesn't like me, and I don't blame him. Most of the time I don't like myself." She glanced down at her steaming mug and then back up at Josie. "How much do you know about him and me?"

Josie shrugged. "He's never said a lot. He seems to keep his cards close to his chest."

"That's one way of putting it." Savannah frowned, lost in thought. "Bear and I were never friends."

"I can't believe that. I'm sure he was nice in the beginning. But after all these years, I imagine it's hard to remember what those early days were like."

"Oh, it's not hard to remember. We were insatiable. We were constantly, you know, every which way, every time we were together. He couldn't get enough of me, and I loved it. I loved him."

"But you stopped loving him."

Savannah lifted her mug. "I don't think one ever stops loving someone like Bear. He gets under your skin, you know?"

"But you ended the relationship."

Savannah arched a brow. "He said that?"

"He's said almost nothing, other than, when it ended between you two, you essentially had the last word."

"I usually do." Savannah smiled grimly. "But the ending of us was brutal. Not just on him, either. It was brutal for me, too. I loved him. We were going to get married and start a family—" She broke off, swallowed, her throat working. "But it didn't work out that way."

"You couldn't accept the paralyzed Bear?"

"*He* couldn't accept the paralyzed Bear. I know you've only ever known this Bear, the one in a chair, but it was hard for Bear to go from being one thing and then another. *My* Bear wasn't broken. He wasn't a paraplegic. He'd always been on top, a winner, a champion. Nothing stopped him. He rode with injuries, broken arms, broken collarbones, injured legs, knees, hips. He rode with cracked ribs and collapsed lungs—"

"That's terrible. Truly."

Savannah's shoulders rose and fell. "It was his choice, and his career. Bear has always known who he was, and understands better than anyone his identity, his value, and his appeal to audiences. Bear Anderson. Champion bull rider. Montana myth."

Josie nodded, aware that Savannah was speaking the truth. Or his truth. Bear was his own person. He wasn't one that could be manipulated or pushed. Which couldn't have been easy for Savannah following the accident. "I can only imagine how awful it was after he was hurt."

"It was. We had a difficult time figuring out our way forward. I don't know how to talk about it still. It was so complicated and so heartbreaking, and I made some decisions that changed everything. As if everything hadn't already been changed."

That mocking note was back in Savannah's voice, but Josie was learning that Savannah wasn't poking fun at Josie, but rather mocking herself. Bear did that, too. They must have been one powerful, formidable couple.

"I'm sorry if I sounded critical," Josie said. "I don't mean to judge. I probably put the facts together and got it wrong."

"I doubt you have it wrong. And if Bear hasn't told you the truth, I will. When he was in his coma I ended my pregnancy. With his baby. We were engaged, and the doctors prepared me for the worst. They said it was unlikely he'd make it, and if he did, he wouldn't be the same. So, I did what I thought was best for both of us."

Josie had not known any of this, and she fought to hide her shock and revulsion. "But then he survived," she said.

"He did. He was paralyzed. He had significant trauma. The next six to nine months were incredibly difficult."

"At what point did you tell him you were no longer pregnant?"

"I didn't tell him. Not initially, but that's because he never knew I was pregnant. It was still early on, and I didn't want to be a pregnant bride, and so I was in a bit of denial, thinking I'd tell him when the time was right, wondering if we should do a quickie courthouse wedding, and then have our big wedding with the family and friends later, after the baby was born. Then he was hurt, and I made the decision to terminate the pregnancy, deciding to never tell him, thinking it was best for him not to know."

"Yet you told him."

"I'd never kept secrets from him. I mean, I've kept secrets from lots of people, but never from Bear. We were always honest with each other, even when it sucked, but that honesty was a big part of what kept us together. Then suddenly I had this huge secret, and then two secrets—the pregnancy and the abortion. It was killing me. Eating me alive. I'd even gone to see a therapist about it, trying to wrap my head around the guilt, as well as the anger that my Bear was gone, and I was struggling to accept that he and I would never be the same. Not as we were."

"Change is brutal."

"And this was impossible." Savannah pushed her tea away from her, palms pressed flat on the counter. "We had a huge fight one day. It had been brewing for a week or more. We were both frustrated and deeply unhappy, and Bear snapped at me, said something about me liking my fans more than him, and it just made me flip. I'd been trying so hard to be positive and cheerful for Bear, putting on a happy face for the rest of the world, and when he attacked me, I just let him have it. I shouted at him that it was a good thing we didn't have the baby because he couldn't even take care of himself." She chewed on her lip a moment. "Of course, he asked what baby?" She shrugged. "I told him."

"Oh, no."

"Oh, yes." Savanah tried to smile but failed. "A lot of things were said, terrible appalling things, the most hurtful upsetting things, and that was pretty much that. The end."

"You haven't forgiven yourself for what you said."

"I haven't forgiven myself for any of it. What I said, what I did. Bear can never have children now. I took his one chance at being a father away from him. I did that. Because I'm a selfish, horrible human being."

Josie struggled to swallow around the lump filling her throat. She wanted to comfort Savannah, but she didn't know what to say. She felt for Bear. She grieved for him. But she also felt Savannah's pain. Savannah was still in a hell of her own making.

As if reading Josie's mind, Savannah added with a laugh, "And now here I am pregnant again, and once again, with no baby daddy." Her eyes shone with tears. "God really does have a funny sense of humor."

Josie swallowed around the lump filling her throat. Twice Savannah had been put in an impossible situation while pregnant, and while Bear had survived his accident, Noah hadn't. Noah wasn't coming back.

Savannah reached down and shaped the loose fabric of her blouse to her tummy, showing up the bump. "I don't know what I'm going to do. I'm not going to end the pregnancy, but I don't think I can keep the baby. I'm not prepared to be a single mom. Besides, it would end my career. Country fans might embrace a bad boy, but they don't love a bad girl."

Josie blinked, touched and moved. No wonder Savannah was here, camping out at houses, looking for a safe haven. What she needed wasn't just a place to stay, she needed a friend. Josie leaned over and hugged Savannah hard before letting her go.

Savannah's eyes were watering when she glanced at Josie. "What was that for?"

"Everybody needs friends," Josie said fiercely.

"Yes, but not everybody deserves them." And then Savannah winked and slid off the stool. "I'm going to go to bed, but I think you and Bear have unfinished business. My gut says you have more talking to do. There's something he's not telling you, but he should. He owes you the truth, and not whatever bullshit explanation he gave you tonight."

BEAR COULDN'T SLEEP. He felt sick, physically and emotionally ill.

He hated what he'd said to Josie today. He hated what he'd done. He hated cutting her loose and pushing her away when everything in him wanted to keep her close.

It had been nearly impossible to say those things to her, and he'd hardened himself against her before leaving his room to speak to her. As he'd talked, he'd steeled himself against the hurt in her expression. He'd steeled himself from caring, because in his heart, he knew he was doing what was best for her.

Josie couldn't see it now, but one day she'd be glad. She was only twenty-three, and one day she'd be glad he'd protected her, saving her for someone who would give her the life she deserved. Josie deserved the best. She deserved someone who would look out for her and put her first. Bear knew he couldn't.

Not because he wouldn't want to, but his accident had changed everything about him, giving him an injury that required constant vigilance. His paralysis meant he had to think for his body. He had to keep track of things most able-bodied men didn't. When had he last used a bathroom? How long had he been sitting? Had he checked his skin lately? Were there any bruises? Any sores? Anything that could be a problem? He had to scrutinize himself the way most men would never have to scrutinize, and the last thing he wanted to do was turn Josie—beautiful, brilliant, passionate Josie—into his nurse. That was her sister's calling. Not Josie's.

But that didn't make this easy. There wasn't always joy in doing the right thing. And letting Josie find her future with someone else was the right thing, but it sure hurt like hell.

BEAR'S TRUCK WAS in the driveway when Josie drove to the house to begin packing all of her things. She'd parked at the curb but hesitated to turn the engine off. What if he was here? But what if he wasn't, and it was just his truck here?

"I thought you were leaving for Texas."

"My flight was delayed. I'm heading out this afternoon now."

"I'll come back then," she said, retreating to the door.

He didn't argue. He silently watched her start to go but at the last moment Josie turned around in the doorway. "Why are you so sure you are wrong for me?" she asked, facing him.

"Because I can't give you everything you need. It's as simple as that."

"You're talking about sex—"

"Yes, I'm talking about sex, but not just about sex. I'm talking about mobility and lifespan. Talking about struggles and hassles that will be with me forever. There is no healing an injury like mine. Why should you have to go through any of that if you don't have to? Why should you be burdened with the problems I have?

"This is just so crazy. You've never talked like this to me—"

"But I thought it. Many times."

"And is that why you were determined to keep me at arm's length? Is that why the idea of kissing me was so awful? Why you were doing your best to treat me like a sister? No romance for fear that I would fall for you? Well news alert, Bear Anderson, I fell for you the first day I met you. So, there's that."

"I do compare you to Susie. You are right. And I wouldn't want Susie to ever have less in life. I wouldn't want her to date someone—or fall in love with someone—who was like me. I would do everything in my power to convince her to hold out for more, for better. Just like I want better for you."

Josie shook her head, a slow, frustrated defiant shake of her head. "Can we just turn this around for a minute?"

"You can't. Josie, I know what I'm dealing with, and I know what I've been through, and I know what will happen down the road—"

"I'm not Savannah, Bear. Maybe she couldn't handle the challenges, but I can. I was there when Jasper was born, and I have been there on the nights that no one thought he'd survive, and we got through it as a family—"

"But I'm not your family."

"But Susie is."

"Yes."

"And you said you wouldn't want her to date someone like you, or to get serious with someone like you."

"Yes. And I mean it."

"Okay, but what if Susie was the one hurt? What if Susie was injured? Your beautiful, warm, loving, lovely sister who made the family laugh? Who has been there for you when you were at her lowest. What if she was in an accident, and paralyzed—"

"*Don't.*"

"Hear me out, Bear. What if she was single and her mind was all there, and her body was there, but due to a spinal cord injury, she was paralyzed. Would you want loving, strong men to avoid her? Would you scare off the good guys? Would you think she deserved less than she did before she was hurt?"

"Of course not."

"Would you think Susie is just half of a woman now, so

she only gets half of the man?"

"No. Never. She'd still be Susie."

"Exactly." Josie burned with anger, her hands knotted at her sides "You'd still want the best for her. You love her. You're proud of who she is and the woman she's become, and you'd want someone wonderful for her, someone who sees her as you do. And I see you. I don't see what doesn't work in you. I just see you, who you are, and who you have always been. But I also can't make you love me, and if that's really the issue here … you don't love me … then you're right. Let me go. Because that's the only way I can leave you. It's the only way I can give up on us."

JOSIE HELD HIS gaze so long that Bear's insides hurt, his chest tight, his gut filled with bits of broken glass. He didn't want to lie to her. He wasn't a man who liked dishonesty, but the truth would keep her here, tethered to him, and that was exactly what he couldn't do.

"I don't love you the way I should," he said after an endless silence. "I'm sorry, Josie, I really am."

Her features crumpled; her shoulders slumped. "You mean that, don't you?"

"I do."

Chapter Sixteen

IF AUGUST HAD been the best month of Josie's life, then September was the worst. She moved back to her parents' home outside Bozeman because she couldn't bear to remain in Marietta. She was sorry to give up her job at the gallery, but just driving down Main Street gave Josie pain.

Her parents were happy to have her home, and Josie applied for jobs in downtown Bozeman since she needed work, and since she'd achieved what she needed to do with Bear's business for her design project to be accepted by her advisor, Josie was essentially done with school.

It was strange to have so much to do and then suddenly to be at loose ends. No one was hiring, either, at least, not work she was excited to do. Her dad told her to take some time for herself. He said she'd worked hard her entire life and it was okay for her to just rest a bit.

It was good advice but Josie couldn't rest. She couldn't relax. She couldn't eat, or sleep, or focus on anything. Everything in her felt bruised. Broken. But maybe it's because her heart was broken.

Marietta was in the past, and Bear was too, not that she could forget him just because she'd moved home. He seemed to always be there in her thoughts, and her heart, but their last conversation had been so brutal that she could only pick up the pieces of her heart and move forward.

Rye and Ansley brought Mick with them when they came to visit. They seemed as happy as always, and Mick absolutely favored Ansley, sitting at her side, and following her wherever she went.

Mick's devotion to Ansley made Josie smile. Clearly Mick knew a good human when he saw one. But before Rye and Ansley left during their last visit, Ansley drew Josie aside. "You're losing too much weight," she said to Josie, giving her a quick hug. "You need to make sure you're getting some protein and healthy food in you."

"I just can't eat," Josie answered. "I can't chew or swallow. It's like there's a rock inside my throat."

"Would it make you feel any better to know that Bear isn't doing very well, either?"

"No." Josie blinked back tears. "I wouldn't want to wish this feeling on my worst enemy."

Ansley gave Josie another hug. "I hate that you're going through this. But it will get better. I promise."

Josie patted her sister-in-law's back. "I'm holding you to that."

THAT EVENING AS Rye drove back to Marietta, he held

Ansley's hand, grateful to have her at his side. "That was not fun tonight," he said. "I hate seeing Josie like that."

"I know."

"I'm not sure that living at home is the best thing for her. She seems like a shadow of herself."

"Don't you think she'd be just as sad if she was living alone?"

He sighed. "Maybe."

Ansley said nothing for the next couple of miles and then brought up a subject that had been on her mind for the past few days. "My brother Lachlan saw your mom and Bear Anderson having coffee together a couple weeks ago." Ansley crossed her legs, but still couldn't get comfortable. "Were you aware of this?"

Rye glanced at her. "Bear and Mom?"

Ansley nodded. "In Livingston."

"Why Livingston?"

"I don't know, but it seems really strange, because from what Lachlan said, Jennifer and Bear met for coffee right around the time Bear asked Josie to move out."

Rye's foot came off the accelerator. "Was Lachlan sure it was them?"

"He's pretty good with faces, particularly when it's your sister's lookalike sitting with Bear Anderson. I mean, it's hard to confuse Bear for anyone else."

"It doesn't make sense. The two of them meeting, never mind meeting in Livingston where neither one lives."

Ansley put her hand on her husband's knee. "Which would make it a great place to meet if you didn't want anyone to know you were meeting."

"You've been watching too many of your crime shows," he said, but there was no sting in his words, just worry.

"Think about it, Rye. They met the day of, or the day before, Bear asked Josie to move out." Ainsley's brow furrowed. "I can't help wondering if that coffee meet-up had something to do with the fallout between Bear and Josie. Because up until then, everything seemed to be going really well. We had dinner with them several times, we went to a movie, went to Flintworks, went for ice cream with them. And never once was there anything weird or awkward. Nothing to indicate that Bear would ask Josie to leave."

"My mom would never interfere. I don't see it happening."

"You're sure? Because I remember how she wasn't thrilled about me. I remember how when you and I were having some trouble she wanted me to leave. She thought it was in your best interest for me to go. If it hadn't been for your sisters, I don't think we would have figured this out."

Rye said nothing and Ansley felt a pang. "I'm not blaming your mom, but I am grateful for your sisters. They were the ones who got us together. Your mom had serious reservations."

"I do remember," he said roughly. Rye drummed his fingers on the steering wheel. "You don't think Bear might have been the one to invite Mom to coffee? You don't think he wanted to get to know her better?"

"If that were the case, why would he tell Josie almost immediately after that she needed to move out? I mean, would he reach out to your mom—of all people—and give her a heads-up, saying, 'Hey I'm about to break your daughter's heart, just wanted you to know?'" Ansley shrugged. "Because I would think if that were the case your mom would have said something to Josie. She would have prepared her. She would not have let Josie walk into something like that blind."

Rye slowly nodded. "You think Mom asked Bear to meet her."

"I do."

"And you think Mom had an agenda?"

Ansley took her time answering, knowing she needed to pick her words with care. "I think your mom was worried that Bear would hurt her. And I think she warned him off first."

Rye said nothing, taking it in.

"I'd say let them sort it out," Ansley added after a moment. "But Josie said something to me tonight when we were doing the dishes, and I'm not sure if she's serious. She's thinking of going away, moving out of state."

"Josie would never leave Montana."

"That's not what she said tonight."

Rye shot his wife a narrowed glance. "Is she just being

dramatic?"

"I don't know. If she were in the right headspace, I'd think going somewhere new was a good idea, but, honey, she's in so much pain. I'm worried about her."

"She's tougher than she looks."

"Oh, I don't doubt that. But if your mom has said something, or possibly interfered, is it right for us to stand by and do nothing?"

DAYS PASSED WHILE Rye deliberated over what should be done, at first thinking he couldn't involve himself, and then changing his mind, and thinking as the oldest, he couldn't ignore the situation. Perhaps something had to be said, only he wasn't sure who to speak to first—his mom or Bear. He suspected neither would be particularly forthcoming. His mom would be downright defensive. Maybe even overly emotional, too.

Aware that he had a meeting with Bear scheduled at the Fuller Building Friday morning, Rye decided that after they covered business, he'd ask Bear if he'd met with Mom, and what that conversation had been about.

The meeting Friday didn't take long. Rye's subs were on top of things, and the interior was taking shape with electrical and plumbing both in, and drywalling to come next. Bear had no complaints about the job progress, but then, he had virtually nothing to say. Bear was silent and stoic and clearly eager to escape.

Rye told Bear there was one more thing to discuss, but he'd like to go outside for this conversation.

Bear's expression turned wary, but he rolled out onto the street where he pivoted to face Rye. "I have another meeting in a half hour," he said, voice flat, devoid of emotion. "Just so you know."

"Not a problem. This shouldn't take long," Rye answered, but then he hesitated. This was not easy, and Bear had never been more remote or detached. "I know you and my mom met in Livingston. Either the same day, or the day before you and Josie had your falling out. I wondered if you ever told Josie that you met with Mom, and if she was aware of everything that had happened."

Bear just stared at Rye.

"These are small towns," Rye said. "Livingston isn't all that far from where my parents now live."

Bear still kept silent.

"Ansley thinks Mom asked you to meet her. I didn't want to believe it, but after thinking it over, Ansley is probably right. You don't have to tell me what Mom wanted to discuss with you, but I think you should share that information with Josie. It doesn't seem right that a lot of people now know, and the one person that should know, doesn't."

"Your mom wants what is best for your sister," Bear said,

breaking his silence.

"We all do."

"Which is why Josie and I are pursuing different paths and opportunities."

"You were never an opportunity, Bear. You were the person she loved." Rye's throat thickened with emotion. "Josie isn't a romantic. She doesn't walk around in a fantasy world. As far as I know, until you, she's never been in love."

Bear averted his face. "Don't say that."

"She loves you. Really, truly loves you. And if you have any feelings for her, you'd fill her in on what happened, so she'd at least know. So she could at least accept that change in your behavior. As it is, she's blaming herself."

"She did nothing wrong. She's pretty much perfect."

"Then reassure her before she leaves. Let her head off to her new life with some peace. That is, if you care for her, at all."

"Where is she going? When is she going?"

"Soon, Ansley said. Probably in the next week or two."

SHOWING UP UNINVITED to the Calhouns was not something Bear looked forward to, but if Rye was right, and Josie was leaving, Bear had to speak to her. He'd tried to call her, but his calls went unanswered. He'd texted her, too, but again, nothing. He began to wonder if she'd possibly blocked his number. It would be one way of dealing with him. An effective way of ensuring he could no longer bother her.

He parked in the driveway and unloaded his chair, and as he did so, he saw a curtain move in one of the windows. It looked like Josie, but then it could have been Jennifer.

A moment later, the front door opened and Jennifer was walking out, heading toward him.

"Good afternoon," he greeted Mrs. Calhoun politely.

"Can I help you, Bear?"

"Yes. Could you ask Josie to come outside? I'd like to talk to her. It won't take long."

"She's working with Jasper right now. They're doing some of his exercises that are part of his physical therapy."

"That's okay. I'm happy to wait. I'll be just out here, reading on my phone until she's done."

"Bear—I mean, Braden—"

"Bear's fine."

Jennifer stepped closer, her voice dropping. "I don't know that there is anything that needs to be said between you and Josie. I think everything that was important has been said."

"That's probably true, but I'd still like to say goodbye, before she leaves."

"Where is she going?"

"She's planning on moving. She told Ansley she needs to go, and it's probably soon, so I'll just wait until she's free so I can wish her well and tell her to travel safely."

A side gate opened, and Josie walked out, her long dark hair in a low ponytail, and her sweatpants baggy and hanging off her lean hips. "Dad told me you were here," she said, walking toward Bear and her mom. "He suggested I come out and see if everything was alright." Her gaze darted from one to the other. "Is everything alright?"

"Yes," Jennifer said.

Bear shook his head. "No."

"Bear," Jennifer interjected with a tense smile.

Bear ignored her, focusing only on Josie. "Can we go for a drive? I can have you back in twenty minutes or so."

Josie hesitated and then nodded.

It took a few minutes for Bear to transfer back into the truck and stow away his chair but then they were off. They didn't speak until they'd been traveling a mile or so.

"I understand you're thinking about moving," he said, breaking the silence, his gaze fixed on the road.

"Who told you?"

"Rye."

"I imagine Ansley told him." She sighed and tucked a long tendril of hair behind her ear. "But they're right. I am going. I'm hoping to be gone early next week."

Bear flexed his fingers, then forced himself to relax. "Any idea of where you're going to go?"

"Seattle, and then Portland, and then depending on how I feel, I might drive down the coast all the way to San Diego."

"Why?"

"I've never been to the West Coast. I've never seen much of anything. Both you and Rye have done a lot of traveling and it's my turn to see some of the world."

"Your family will miss you." Bear glanced at Josie's profile. There was no light in her eyes, no hope or warmth, either. "If they missed Hannah who is only in Missoula, I can't imagine how they will handle you so far away."

"Maybe it'll be good for them." She smiled grimly. "Maybe it will teach them to mind their own business."

He drew a slow breath, trying to calm his nerves. "So you know."

"More than everyone thinks I know." She glanced at him, her expression cool.

His lashes dropped. "Has something happened?"

She gave him a long cool look. "You tell me. It seems like we were doing well until you and my mom had coffee. That must have been some crazy coffee for you to kick me out of your house. Practically the same day."

"Your mom gave me a lot to think about. She made me realize that you are young, and you have dreams, and it wasn't fair to trap you—"

"Stop," she cried, hitting the dashboard. "Let me out. I'd rather walk home than listen to this. It's insulting, Bear."

Bear braked hard and pulled over to the side of the narrow ranch road. "I have no desire to insult you."

"You know, for a smart man, you can be incredibly stupid. Trapped? *Trapped with you*? Trapped with the man I adored? The man I admired? The man I loved? How is that trapped?"

"There are other men who could probably give you—"

"No!" she cried, cutting him short. "I can't do this again. Can't listen to this again." She turned on the seat and faced him. "If this is indeed our last conversation ever, be straight with me. Respect me enough to tell me the truth."

"What do you want to know?"

"Why did you meet Mom?"

"She called and asked me to."

"And you didn't think you should tell me?"

"I wasn't sure what to think."

"And what did she tell you when you met for coffee?" Josie's voice cracked. "It certainly couldn't have been complimentary."

"She wanted better for you. More for you. And after thinking about it—"

"In your bedroom, in the dark?"

"She was right. You deserve the world, and I can't give it to you."

Tears filled Josie's eyes. "Did I ever ask for the world? How did I overwhelm you with my needs?"

"No. You didn't."

"Then why kick me out like that? Why treat me like I was nothing … like I was garbage on trash day?"

"It wasn't like that, Josie. It was never like that. I love

you, but my love won't be enough."

"Says who? My mom? My dad? Rye?"

"This isn't about them. It's about you and me."

"Yes, it is. So, you kicked me out because you don't—and can't—love me. That's what you said the next morning when I returned to the house. That you don't love me. That you'll never feel the way I feel for you." Her furious gaze held his. "Is that true?"

"No." He swallowed, shook his head. "That was a lie."

"What are the other lies?"

"I don't know if there are other lies. I just know that I did not want to fall in love with you, that I resisted loving you, but I couldn't help loving you. I've loved you for months. I love everything about you."

"And you believe there is someone else out there who is better for me?"

He ground his jaw together, teeth grinding.

"We're being honest with each other, Bear. Tell me. Do you believe someone can love me better than you?"

"Physically, yes. Emotionally, no."

"So, this is about sex."

"It's about sex and parenthood. It's about what I can't do—"

"But what about the things you can? What about your heart? What is wrong with that? Is it somehow damaged, too?"

He looked away, his chest on fire, his gut sharp with

pricks of pain. "I can't give you all the reasons why someone else can love you better, Josie, because I don't know if anyone else could ever love you better than me. But what do I know? I'm all tangled up. When it comes to you, I have no clarity. I care so much for you it hurts. When you're away from me, it hurts. When I think about you leaving and going halfway across the country I can hardly breathe. Your mom begged me to put you first and I'm trying. But Josie"—he turned his head, looked at her, unable to hide the tears in his eyes—"how am I supposed to be okay when you're my heart?"

Josie knocked away tears of her own. "Mom shouldn't have gotten involved. She should never put that guilt trip on you. Because it was a guilt trip. She acted as if I was some crazy codependent daughter who had no will of her own, no boundaries, no healthy sense of self. But my mom was wrong. I didn't show up for my dad because I had to. I showed up for my dad because I *wanted* to. There's a difference. I didn't remain close to my family because I lacked confidence. I was close to them because I was strong enough to handle their craziness and demands." She patted her chest hard. "I've always known who I am. I've always known what I wanted to do. I've known since I was a little girl that I was put here to do good, to help others, to shine a light where I could. That's not because I am empty and hollow. It's because I'm focused. Determined."

He bowed his head, closed his eyes, unable to feel so

much pain and pressure.

"Bear," Josie moved toward him, putting her hand on his thigh. "Look at me."

He did.

She reached up to touch his cheekbone, his jaw, her touch light and tender. "I didn't fall in love with you because I pitied you. I fell in love with you because I admired you, and respected you, and went all weak whenever you looked at me. I loved your face and your smile, the set of your shoulders and those scars wrapping your arm, earning you the name Bear."

It hurt to breathe. His chest was raw. Josie kept using the word *loved*. Not love. She'd loved him. But was it over? Was she done?

"What made me really want you, though," she continued, "wasn't your face or your laughter or anything superficial. What I loved was your determination to do for others, your determination to give back. You decided to take what you've earned and do something important with it and I couldn't be prouder. Your goals became my goals. Your dreams echoed my own. They didn't replace mine. They felt like mine. You see, we both had wanted the same thing."

Have I lost you, Josie? The words were there on the tip of his tongue, but he couldn't speak, couldn't say them.

"Tell me, Bear, why was it so wrong for me to admire you? You don't drink. You don't do drugs. You don't lose your temper. You give and ask for nothing. You literally ask for nothing. So why can't I want to give you something? Why can't I give you my heart? Seems like is the least I can do."

"Josie, I don't want you to leave." The husky words were ripped from him, his voice strangled.

"I don't want to leave either, Bear, but I have to. I am livid with my mother. Livid with my father. Why didn't Rye and Ansley come to me sooner and tell me the truth? Why didn't you tell me the truth? I can't do these secrets and games."

"I don't think anyone meant it that way. I think your mom wanted the best for you. Just as your family wants the best for you." *Just as I want the best for you.*

And then it hit him, the problem, the source of all this confusion. Bear didn't know what was best for her. No one did. No one could. Josie was the only one who knew what she needed. And she'd never been consulted.

As if able to read his mind, she added. "My family didn't trust me to make that decision for myself. They couldn't respect that I'd have an opinion, that I would know what I needed. Wanted." She exhaled hard. "Why do people assume that just because I have the capacity to love, that I lack the capacity to think? How can everyone assume that I'm so tenderhearted that it's made me scatterbrained and helpless?"

"I don't know."

"I'm not helpless. I'm not weak. If anything, I am stronger than everyone knows." Her chin lifted. "I can leave here and not look back. I can cut everyone off if I need to prove that I'm an adult and independent and perfectly able to put myself first."

"I'd hate for you to cut everyone off, but yes, you should put yourself first. It's time."

She just looked at him, that small mirthless smile on her lips. It was disconcerting to say the least. Bear flexed his hands on the steering wheel. "What can I do to help you?" he asked, voice pitched quote low. "Is there packing you need done? Any arrangements I can help you with?"

"No, I have everything in control. I'm just working on some logistics, where to stop at night, places to stay, but I'm enjoying the planning. My first solo adventure."

"Were you going to say goodbye?"

She hesitated, lips pursed. "No."

"Why not?"

"Because we already did that. Remember? It about killed me the first time. I've finally recovered and have no interest in going through any of that again."

"So, who is driving west with you?"

"Me."

"That's a long way."

"I'll play some good music."

He struggled to put his feelings into words. The last thing he wanted to do was push her further away. "Should you feel like some company, I'd be happy to ride shotgun. Once in Seattle, I can book a flight home." He hesitated.

"Or hang out and explore with you. I used to love being on the road. It'd be fun to do a road trip with you."

"What about your business?"

"There's nothing I can do until the equipment arrives, and that's at least another three weeks, possibly longer."

Josie's eyes filled with tears, and she looked away. "I've been so upset."

"I don't blame you."

"It was all just so demoralizing." She looked at him now, her pain evident, her emotions still so raw. "My mom was wrong," she added huskily, "but you, you, Bear, were the worst. You kicked me to the curb. You said terrible things."

Bear swallowed around the lump in his throat. "I'm sorry."

"Don't ever do that to me again—regardless of the reason. If you have something to say, be honest with me. Respect me enough to tell me the truth."

"I was trying to protect you, but I know now that I failed."

"You can protect me from the bad guys, but you can't be the bad guy." Her voice broke and the tears were falling again. "I trusted you, Bear. I trusted you more than I've trusted almost anyone."

He tilted up the steering wheel and then reached over and scooped her up, settling her on his lap. His arms went around her, and he just held her to him, held her firmly, held her as though he'd never let her go again.

She turned her face to his chest, finding that spot between his neck and collarbones. He felt her tears on his skin and her breath through the fabric of his shirt. "You said you loved me."

"I do."

"How much?"

"To the moon and back."

She hesitated. "Aren't the stars farther?"

"Then to the stars and back."

"What about the moon, can't it be the stars and the moon—"

"And the sun, and every other galaxy there is. I love you that much, Josie. I love you forever, from now until the end."

She sighed and relaxed against him. "I need you in my life, Bear. We make a good team."

"We make a great team."

Silence stretched. Josie drew a slow breath, her hand against his chest, just above his heart. "Savannah said we weren't done. She said this was a blip and not like you."

He looked down at her in surprise. "You went to Savannah for relationship advice?"

Josie laughed and gave his chest a warm pat. "No. She just happened to be at Rye's house the night you kicked me out. She was a good listener that night. She was there when I needed a friend."

Bear wrestled with his emotions and then smoothed Josie's hair back from her brow and kissed her temple. "I'm glad. I should have been your friend that night. But since I wasn't, I'm glad someone was there. I love you, my sweet Josie. Can we try this again? Is it too late to make it work?"

She snuggled closer. "Never too late. Just like its written in Corinthians. Love is patient, love is kind. Love never fails." She looked up at him. "Our love won't fail, either."

He kissed her lips. "It won't. I promise you that, my heart."

Epilogue

IN ALL, BEAR and Josie spent four weeks on their road trip. They took Bear's Bronco for the trip, so they could both drive. His classic truck had hand controls, as well as the regular foot pedals, so they took turns at the wheel.

Seattle might have been the destination, but they only spent a day there, before driving south to Tacoma and heading west to the Olympic National Park and then the Hoh Rain Forest.

Washington state proved to have excellent accessible trails and they explored the mountains and lush green rain forest on sunny and wet days before continuing south to Portland. From Portland it was another detour to the coast where they stayed in an adorable grey shingle cottage in Cannon Beach for several days.

From Cannon Beach it was down to Northern California—they skipped San Francisco as they both preferred small towns—and visited Monterey and stunning Carmel before doing another detour to Yosemite.

Yosemite was a favorite, not just for the scenery, but for the romance. Bear splurged so they could stay at the grand Ahwahnee Hotel. It was in the historic Ahwahnee's fabled dining room that Bear proposed, presenting her with a stunning Marquise cut diamond he'd bought in Carmel while she'd been answering emails from her Bozeman design firm which hoped to hire her full time.

Josie wasn't sure she wanted to return to work for Melissa and Neil—or anyone else—but she absolutely knew marrying Bear was the right choice, and accepted his proposal with tears in her eyes.

The ring was a little loose on her finger but otherwise it looked perfect on her hand, and it matched the overwhelming love in her heart. She didn't want a long engagement. Josie already felt wedded to Bear and hoped they'd marry soon.

And so, during the drive back to Montana they chose a route that would take them through Nevada where they married in a very sweet little Las Vegas drive-through chapel. It was just them and two strangers as witnesses. There was no dress, no flowers, no music, nothing but them and their love and commitment to each other for the rest of their lives, for richer or poorer, in sickness and in health, and pledging to do for others whatever they could, for as long as they could.

The next day when they climbed in Bear's Bronco and began the twelve-hour drive home to Marietta, Bear flashed Josie a warm, teasing smile. "How does it feel to be Mrs. Anderson?"

She leaned over and kissed his cheek. "Wonderful." She laughed then kissed him again. "I feel like a legend."

The End

Author's Note

Writing about Bear's Heart protagonist Bear Anderson was a privilege. This story wasn't meant to sensationalize the trauma he experienced, but share with readers the challenges and courage required for those with spinal cord injuries.

Thirty years ago, I met a gorgeous man in a wheelchair. He was smart, charming, and witty. I was smitten. We dated, dreamed, and married. Despite the odds, we created two children, my beautiful sons Jake and Ty. For years I researched and wrote about disabilities, abilities, and lifestyle. Over the years, I was asked a lot of questions by strangers, curious about my marriage as well as how one parents in a wheelchair.

I quickly learned that the wheelchair wasn't the obstacle. The real issue was the wear and tear on the body, and the vigilance required to remain healthy.

Medicine has changed in the past thirty years and there are options for couples with spinal cord injuries that didn't exist before. Technological advances continue to improve the quality of life for those with spinal cord injuries, and my former husband generously shared some of the progress happening now.

If I got facts wrong, it is entirely my fault. If I phrased

something that made someone uncomfortable, I was writing from my heart. I am grateful for the years my former husband and I spent together and the sons we made.

I continue to be a passionate believer in universal design, and the importance of creating inclusive environments.

Thank you for reading BEAR'S HEART. I hope you enjoyed it, and as always, if you have thoughts or concerns you can reach me through my social media or at jane@janeporter.com.

Yours,
Jane

Huckleberry Crisp

Prep Time: 20 mins

Cook Time: 30 mins

Filling:

- 6 cups huckleberries (can swap for a mix blackberries, raspberries and/or boysenberries.)
- ½ tsp lemon juice
- 3/4 cup sugar
- 1/3-1/2 c cornstarch or flour
- ½ tsp cinnamon

Crisp Topping:

- 1 cup brown sugar
- 1 cup all-purpose flour
- 1 cup rolled oats
- 1 tsp ground cinnamon
- 1 tsp vanilla
- ½ cup cubed butter (melted butter works too)

Directions

1. Preheat oven to 375 degrees F
2. Lightly grease a 9x13-inch baking pan.
3. For the filling, combine huckleberries and lemon juice in

a bowl. Mix sugar, cornstarch, and cinnamon in a separate bowl. Add to huckleberries and toss lightly until berries are coated. Pour filling into the greased baking pan.

4. For the topping: mix sugar, flour, oats, vanilla, and cinnamon. Add easy and fast- melt butter and stir until clumps begin to form. Spread topping over filling. For traditional crisp, cut butter into oats, sugar, flour mix using a pastry cutter or two knives until crumbly
5. Bake in the preheated oven until golden brown, about 35-45 minutes. Keep an eye on topping. Allow to cool for 15 minutes before serving.

If you enjoyed *Bear's Heart*,
you'll love the other books in…

The Calhouns & Campbells of Cold Canyon Ranch Series

The Calhouns & Campbells of Cold Canyon Ranch bring together two different families, from two very different backgrounds, both coming together in Marietta, Montana as they fall in love and begin new lives.

Book 1: *Take Me Please, Cowboy*

Book 2: *Bear's Heart*

Look for Savannah's story in the new year!

Available now at your favorite online retailer!

More by Jane Porter

The Wyatt Brothers of Montana series

The Wyatt brothers are tough, competitive, and successful on the professional rodeo cowboy circuit. Love has never been a priority, until now.

See the Wyatt Family Tree here!
janeporter.com/extras/the-wyatt-family-tree

Book 1: *Montana Cowboy Romance*
Book 2: *Montana Cowboy Christmas*
Book 3: *Montana Cowboy Daddy*
Book 4: *Montana Cowboy Miracle*
Book 5: *Montana Cowboy Promise*
Book 6: *Montana Cowboy Bride*

Love on Chance Avenue series

See the Wright sisters find love in small town Marietta, Montana

Book 1: *Take Me, Cowboy*
Winner of the RITA® Award for Best Romance Novella
Book 2: *Miracle on Chance Avenue*
Book 3: *Take a Chance on Me*
Book 4: *Not Christmas Without You*

The Taming of the Sheenans series

The Sheenans are six powerful wealthy brothers from Marietta, Montana. They are big, tough, rugged men, and as different as the Montana landscape.

Book 1: *Christmas at Copper Mountain*
Book 2: *The Tycoon's Kiss*
Book 3: *The Kidnapped Christmas Bride*
Book 4: *The Taming of the Bachelor*
Book 5: *A Christmas Miracle for Daisy*
Book 6: *The Lost Sheenan's Bride*

Paradise Valley Ranch Series

Historical romances

Book 1: *Away in Montana*
Book 2: *Married in Montana*

Love at Langley Park series

Spend Christmas in the charming English countryside with the Roberts sisters

Book 1: *Once Upon a Christmas*
Book 2: *The Christmas Cottage*

Other Titles

Oh, Christmas Night
The Tycoon's Forced Bride
The Frog Prince

Available now at your favorite online retailer!

About the Author

New York Times and USA Today bestselling author of 70 romances and fiction titles, **Jane Porter** has been a finalist for the prestigious RITA award six times and won in 2014 for Best Novella with her story, *Take Me, Cowboy*, from Tule Publishing. Today, Jane has over 13 million copies in print, including her wildly successful, *Flirting With Forty*, which was made into a Lifetime movie starring Heather Locklear, as well as *The Tycoon's Kiss* and *A Christmas Miracle for Daisy*, two Tule books which have been turned into holiday films for the GAC Family network. A mother of three sons, Jane holds an MA in Writing from the University of San Francisco and makes her home in sunny San Clemente, CA with her surfer husband and three dogs.

Thank you for reading

Bear's Heart

If you enjoyed this book, you can find more from all our great authors at TulePublishing.com, or from your favorite online retailer.

Printed in Great Britain
by Amazon